"You heal quic
trembling as she

"Maybe your kis
before he could bit

"What?" She stared at him, her eyes full of anger and uncertainty. "I thought you were too delirious to remember that," she said in a soft voice.

"I don't forget when someone like you kisses me."

She flared beautifully. "I didn't kiss you, you kissed me." She slapped the new dressing down on his leg, then dragged the blanket back over him. "Or more accurately, you kissed someone you called Mai-Lee. If you hadn't been injured and burning up with fever, I'd have clocked you one."

"Mai-Lee lies a long way back in my past," he said, taking her hand. "Not as far back as you do, though. And if I kissed her instead of you in my delirium, I'd better remedy that. Every woman deserves to be kissed for her own sake." Besides, he thought, studying her flushed cheeks and furious green eyes, he wanted to kiss Shell Landry again.

"Who are you, and what have you come here for? What do you want?" she asked, trying to pull free.

"Want?" he asked, drawing her closer to him. "I want to get to know you again. I've come to stake a claim. . . ."

WHAT ARE *LOVESWEPT* ROMANCES?

They are stories of true romance and touching emotion. We believe those two very important ingredients are constants in our highly sensual and very believable stories in the *LOVESWEPT* line. Our goal is to give you, the reader, stories of consistently high quality that may sometimes make you laugh, sometimes make you cry, but are always fresh and creative and contain many delightful surprises within their pages.

Most romance fans read an enormous number of books. Those they truly love, they keep. Others may be traded with friends and soon forgotten. We hope that each *LOVESWEPT* romance will be a treasure—a "keeper." We will always try to publish

LOVE STORIES YOU'LL NEVER FORGET
BY AUTHORS YOU'LL ALWAYS REMEMBER

The Editors

Loveswept ®575

Judy Gill
Forbidden Dreams

BANTAM BOOKS
NEW YORK · TORONTO · LONDON · SYDNEY · AUCKLAND

FORBIDDEN DREAMS

A Bantam Book / October 1992

One

Wham! Wham! Wham!

Shell jumped at the first kick on the door and was on her feet when the second one struck. She had her hand on the knob in time for the third, and with her black Labrador beside her, opened the door before the fourth one landed.

"Ned, take it easy," she said with a laugh, ducking her head against the lash of rain-laden wind off the bay. The relentless surf pounded on the tiny gravel beach, and the harsh tang of the roiled ocean came strong. "You didn't need to come out on a night like"—she stepped back involuntarily—"this," she finished in a whisper. She stared up at the tall figure—who was definitely not Ned—standing on her threshold, clutching the doorframe with both hands and swaying as if the wind had him in its teeth and was about to blow him over.

"Oh!" She closed her hand into the thick fur at

Skeena's nape. "I thought you were Ned with an armload of firewood. He brings me some every night about this time and . . . What can I do for—"

The man pitched face-first into the room.

Shell tried to catch him, but his weight was too much. She did little more than break his fall before she let him collapse, his upper body lying on the rag rug.

Skeena growled low in her throat as she stood wary, watchful, her ruff straight up.

Shell stared at the recumbent man, noticing with surprise that he wore no shoes, just very wet, tattered socks that showed a bloody scrape on the sole of his right foot. Even as she watched, rain sluiced over that foot, diluting the blood, soaking it into the once-white sock before fresh blood welled up. Bending, she grasped his shoulders and skidded him and the rug along the hardwood floor, farther into the room. When he was all the way in, she shut the door, closing out the wildness of the December night.

Shell grabbed the oil lamp from the desk where she'd been going over book catalogs and hunkered beside the man, holding the lamp high. In its glow she saw that the back of his jeans and jacket were coated in mud, but other than the cut foot, she discerned no injury. With faint amazement she realized she'd expected to see something horrible, like a bullet wound. Lord, she'd been watching too much television, reading too many thrillers. Spies didn't exist in coastal British Columbia as far as she knew. Although, she thought, frowning, drug dealers had been known to die violently even in remote areas. She also noticed with the same detached amazement that her hands shook as she slid one around his neck, seeking a pulse in his throat.

It beat steadily. His skin was warm inside the collar of his jacket, warmer than she'd anticipated. That suggested he hadn't been washed ashore from a shipwreck, though his jeans and jacket were surely wet enough for him to have swum all the way from Vancouver Island.

He groaned, rose up as far as his elbows, and turned his head from side to side as if testing his neck. Skeena growled again, and he peered at the dog before slumping back down, his eyes closed. He appeared not to have noticed Shell.

"Wake up." Her voice was as sharp as her finger and thumb pinching his earlobe. She remembered reading somewhere—likely in a spy novel—that a good pinch there would make a faker flinch. He didn't flinch. More gently, she prodded him with one hand until he moaned and opened his eyes, focusing on her with difficulty.

He muttered a single syllable that had the intonation of a question, and she answered as best she could. "You're safe. You're in my house. I'll help you."

"Sh-ell?"

She started. Shell? Had he said her name? Of course not. There was no way this stranger could possibly know her name. The state he was in, it would be a miracle if he knew his own. But what if he wasn't a stranger? His face was half-obscured by a thick swatch of dark hair that tumbled over his forehead and temple, and a five o'clock shadow that had reached ten o'clock. Nevertheless, she was sure she didn't know him.

"Can you turn over?" she asked. "Are you hurt?"

He mumbled something more, then with great effort managed to help her as she rolled him to his back. The action clearly caused him intense pain, because his face creased and his lips pulled back, baring his teeth. His front was as liberally smeared with mud as his back, as if he'd been wallowing in a swamp. His lack of shoes supported that supposition, but Shell wasted little time wondering where he'd been. Blood poured from a gash high on his left thigh, and he covered it with a hand as he groaned.

"All right," she said, sweeping the flaring skirt of her flannel granny gown aside and inching closer on her knees. "Let me look." She gently pried his fingers away from the injury. Wet, torn denim clung to his leg, dark and sticky where blood had soaked the fabric. She set the lamp down to grasp the cloth in both hands, enlarging the tear. Holding the lamp up again, she saw an ugly wound, long, deep, gaping wide at one end, and bleeding thickly.

For a second the lamp trembled in her hand, and the man raised his own hand to steady it.

"Easy, Florence," he said with a weak chuckle, which surprised her. If she had a wound like that, she wouldn't be laughing. His chuckle didn't last long, though. He tried to sit up, then flopped back down, grimacing with pain, one arm wrapped around his chest. His eyes fell shut, and his head flopped to one side.

"Lie still," she said unnecessarily, because he appeared to be unconscious. Damn! The hard planes and angles of his face were so white, he looked green. Was he bleeding elsewhere? Internally, maybe? She grabbed a blanket off the back of the sofa and covered him, then snatched up the phone.

Of course it was dead. She'd known that. It had crackled and fallen silent even while she'd tried to call Hydro to say that the power was out, but she'd hoped . . .

The man groaned, and Shell turned, feeling helpless, stupid, incompetent to help him.

His eyes opened and he slowly levered himself up, clutching the front of the bookcase by the door, then the doorknob, then, as she stepped in close, her waist, her shoulder. His hands were large and cold, and she slid herself under his arm, lending her strength. At last, fully on his feet, he swayed, half clinging to her, half leaning on the door. He pressed a hand to his forehead. "Damn head . . ."

Shell glanced at the couch. It was short, more a love seat than a sofa, and it would never do for this man who towered over her now that he was upright. The spare room, of course.

She hesitated, chewing on her lip. Was she out of her mind, bringing a stranger into her house and considering putting him to bed in her guest room? Yet what choice did she have? A storm was raging outside. He was obviously a victim of it, and he needed help. Actually, he needed more help than she could provide, but she was the only one around at the moment.

A few feet away Skeena still stood alert and watchful. Her hackles were no longer up, but she was very much on guard, the muscles under her sleek black fur alive with tension. No, she wasn't alone, Shell decided, and turned the man toward the hallway. With Skeena at her side there wasn't much she wouldn't face.

"Come with me," she said to the man. "You need to lie down."

"Yeah." His voice was thin now, breathy, and he moved very slowly, as if at the end of his strength.

In the spare room, dimly illuminated by the light from the lamp in the hall, Shell continued to prop him while she struggled to get him out of his wet suede jacket. "Okay," she said soothingly when he moaned. "You can lie down soon." She dropped his jacket. It landed on the floor with a sodden thump and was quickly followed by his shirt. Leaving him clinging to the dresser, she flung back the covers on the bed, then unsnapped and unzipped his jeans, exactly as if she made a habit of stripping strange men—or even men she knew. Her silent laugh contained a touch of hysteria.

He was on the point of collapse when she backed him to the bed, hauled his jeans down over his hips, and eased him to a sitting position on the edge of the mattress. She dragged his pants off the rest of the way, cringing when he gasped with pain as they scraped over the wound on his thigh. She murmured an apology, but he didn't seem to hear. His socks resisted removal, but she rolled them down and off his wet, cold, scraped feet, which looked oddly white and vulnerable for their size.

As she helped him swing his legs up and his torso around, he sighed raggedly. When his head connected with the pillow, he covered the top half of his face with one arm. His breathing was shallow, his mouth twisted.

"Got to . . . phone," he muttered as she pulled the sheet over him. "Washout. Tell cops. Warn people."

"The phone's out," she said, carefully draping the covers to leave his injured leg exposed and pulling them free of his abused feet. She peered at him in the shadowy light. "If it wasn't, do you think I wouldn't have called an ambulance already to get you to a hospital, a doctor?"

He let his arm fall from his face and gazed at her. His eyes were dark, brown or possibly black. It was hard to tell in the shadows. "Don't need . . . doctor." He looked stubborn in that moment, and oddly boyish, as if in the next instant his lower lip might jut out and tremble. He also looked . . . familiar?

Shell had to smile. "Yes, you do need a doctor, but I'm afraid I'm all you've got for the moment. So do what I say. Lie still and don't worry. I'll be right back."

His eyes pleaded with her. "Pills. Pocket." His teeth were chattering now as he shivered, and he pressed the fingers and thumb of his left hand to his temples.

A quick search of his jacket produced a stick of gum and a bottle of prescription pain medication, with a rain-soaked label made out to "Ja n ee e" and instructions that they be taken with food or milk.

With an inner lurch of unease she saw that the issuing drugstore was in Los Angeles.

Los Angeles. California. Hollywood. She swallowed dryly and stared at the mostly obliterated name. What was a man from California doing falling through her doorway only weeks before an important anniversary for the entertainment industry?

"*J, a,* blank, blank, *n,*" she whispered. "Jason?" Nothing else seemed to fit.

He groaned again, rolling his head from side to side. She set the pill bottle on the bedside table and darted to the kitchen for a glass of milk.

When she returned, she crouched by the bed and slid a hand under his head. "Jason?" He opened his eyes and didn't dispute the name. "Can you sit up a bit? I've brought you some milk and your pills." He managed to lift his head far enough to swallow, then flopped back down again, his breathing stertorous. His muttered word might have been "Thanks."

Shell swiftly collected the equipment she'd need and scooped up a lamp from the living room before returning to her patient. He appeared to be sleeping, though his breathing was still much too shallow and rapid, as if he weren't getting enough oxygen.

She set a basin of disinfectant-laced water on the dresser, then held the lamp near him as she peeled back the covers. The light showed her how badly bruised his chest was. She was certain he must have broken ribs, possibly even a damaged kidney, judging by the discoloration that wrapped around his chest and disappeared under his back.

"Oh, brother, you really, really need a doc—" she began, then broke off as the light fell fully on his face. She stared at him, recoiling slightly in . . . It wasn't quite recognition, she realized, but it was, again, a sense of familiarity.

She shivered. Some part of her mind associated that face with . . . a camera. *Danger!* The response was immediate and powerful, and sent her staggering back several paces.

Lilianne! Oh, heavens, he was from Los Angeles, and he'd come looking for Lilianne! A flurry of tremors shook her, and she quickly set down the lamp, chewing on her knuckles as she stared at the stranger. What was she going to do? Ned! She had to get Ned. She had to—

No, dammit! Shell clamped down on her moment of pure panic. Don't be an idiot! she told the frightened little girl who still lived inside her. No one's looking for Lilianne.

It was simply that with the approach of the anniversary, she was on edge. Of course. It was surely just that. Except . . .

Except she *had* seen that face before. She was certain. Only where? When? The answer wouldn't come. Quickly, she picked up his wet jeans and, feeling like a thief, searched the pockets for a wallet. She found nothing more than a handful of coins, most of them American, two crushed Canadian fives, and a crumpled credit-card receipt from a gas station. It was so badly waterlogged, little was legible beyond the station's name and its Blaine, Washington, address. Another search of the jacket pockets, both inside and out, turned up only a hotel-room access card, which did nothing to provide identification of its bearer.

Frowning, she dragged a low footstool close to the bed. With the basin of water on the floor by her feet, she began daubing with a soft cloth at the area surrounding the deep cut on his thigh. He didn't stir, even when she gently spread the lips of the wound and used a wet cotton swab to flick out several pieces of grit that were embedded in the livid flesh. Only his short, shallow breaths told her he was still alive.

She shot another glance at his face. Dammit, who was he? Her initial distrust of him had been as instinctive as it was illogical, but this was something more. Like an itch in the back of her mind, the belief that she knew his face persisted, along with the association of it with a camera.

A stronger shiver of unease slithered through her. Could he possibly be one of those curiosity seekers who annually sought answers to the questions about Lilianne? If so, this was the closest anyone had come so far. She cast another uneasy glance at his still, pale face and tried to reject the thoughts, the fears.

He was too young to be someone from her past—at least the past that had involved Lilianne. He wasn't much older than she.

Forcing the worry away, she concentrated on taking care of his injuries. Finally satisfied that the wound was as clean as she could get it, she dried the skin around it, then drew its edges shut with butterfly strips. As hard as she tried to control it, though, her mind insisted on humming along frantically, trying to sort this all out.

She kept coming up against the same blank wall, however. The man was not old enough to have been one of the horde of photographers and reporters who had poked and prodded and questioned her during her early childhood to the point where she actually became nauseated. Yet her linking his face with a camera seemed to suggest he had been behind some of those exploding flashbulbs she'd so hated.

She bathed his feet and saw that all the scratches, except for one, were superficial. She was being irrational, she told herself. Of course she'd never seen him before. He was a total stranger and no danger to anyone, and he hadn't said her name. That had been a figment of her imagination. More likely, he'd slurred the words "What the hell" or something similar.

It wasn't until she drizzled disinfectant onto the jagged scrape on his right foot that he showed any sign of distress, and then he gasped only once in pain. She bit her lip and glanced at him. His eyes were open, and he was looking at her with a disconcerting intensity. She murmured an apology but continued cleaning the cut until he lifted a hand and touched her hair, shoving it back from her face.

"You . . . hard lady . . . track down," he said, then managed a ghost of a smile. "Shirley Elizabeth Landry, all growed up."

Shell leaped to her feet. A loud, crashing roar filled her ears as her world tilted the wrong way on its axis, then shuddered and fell.

• • •

When Jase fully regained his senses, he realized first that he was warm. He was lying on a bed, and the scent of woodsmoke hung in the air. Something else, familiar and poignant, teased his nostrils as the sensation of fingers, warm and gentle on the skin of his inner thigh, teased his body with a delicate stimulation he wished he could ignore. He could not; it pumped through him, heated his blood, and had an inevitable effect on his sex.

Even the pain in his ribs, in his leg, and the headache—the awful blinding headache that dogged him wherever he went, pouncing in a sneak attack when he could least afford to accommodate it—couldn't override his body's response to that distinctly feminine touch.

But whose touch? Where was he? He wanted to open his eyes, but the pain in his head made his lids heavy. He sought the inner peace that would allow him to control the pain, and presently it began to ebb. The metallic taste that always accompanied it faded, too, and he breathed a bit easier. A vague memory crossed his mind of a female voice talking about pills and milk, telling him to drink.

Yeah. Right. He'd told her about his medication. He hated taking it. Took it only when forced to. Like on the ferry ride . . . how long ago? Not long enough, probably, but if this was an overdose, he kind of liked it. He drifted, enjoying the easing of the pain, the fluttery fingers on his skin, the warmth and comfort of the room.

As the sharpness of the varying pains in his

body eased, fuzzy, confused thoughts flitted around his mind. He tried to focus them. He had to remember, to bring himself up-to-date, but all he recalled was that ferry, the noise, people talking, kids running and playing; the pain, taking pills washed down with execrable coffee; then driving off, knowing he shouldn't drive with that drug in his system. There'd been an endless dark highway, and he'd peered through heavy rain to glimpse road signs while impatient traffic rode his tailpipe. Then, his turnoff, a dirt road. The bouncing beams of his headlights had ricocheted off trees, more trees than he'd seen in one place for years, and then the sudden gleam of white frothing water immediately before his front wheels. He'd jammed on the brakes, then . . . Then what?

Then suffocation, feeling trapped. His leg had been caught, his foot pinned. He'd struggled to get free, to breathe, feeling pain and confusion, then blessed air. Cold, so cold and wet, he'd walked, fallen, got up and walked again. Trees crashed and branches slammed to the ground all around him, as the wind howled and water smashed into rocks, threatening to reach out and snatch him. He saw a dim light that he sometimes thought was his imagination but followed it anyway, not knowing where it would lead but knowing it was his only hope. Then, finally, warmth, a voice, comfort, and those hands on his naked body.

His *naked* body? He clenched his fists and teeth and opened his eyes.

A woman bent over him, a woman with sleek, shining pale hair that clung to her head and flowed past her shoulders, effectively screening her face from him. He lay on a bed, head and shoulders elevated against thick, soft pillows, in a room all dark except for the intimate glow of an oil lamp standing on a chair next to the woman. He was half-covered by a quilt, and not fully naked after all. He still wore his blue briefs. Intent on her job of bathing his thigh, the woman didn't look at him. That gash . . .

Yes. He had it now. His Jeep and the washout on the road, the road to . . . He frowned, wishing he could think. Ah, yes. The road to Shell Landry's house. Of course.

He was in her house. He'd knocked on the door. Pounded. He remembered a woman snatching it open. Remembered a laughing face turned up to his as she said something. Remembered that laughter dying as she'd stared at him blankly, seeing a stranger.

Then there was nothing.

His gaze wandered around through the pool of yellow light. His pill bottle. He squinted. Yes. She'd given him his medication. That was why the pain was fading, why he was adrift within his head. He tried to focus on his surroundings.

Just within the outer edge of the lamp's glow sat a black Labrador with a broad forehead and intelligent eyes, eyes that watched him with wary intensity. Beyond, through a doorway, he saw the source of the poignant aroma—a Christmas tree—standing in one corner of a room. An old-fashioned rocking chair sat near it, complete with patchwork cushions that reminded him of his grandmother, and on a table was another lamp like the one that lit this room. It was as if he'd stepped through a time warp, he thought, into a much further past than the one that included the child Shell Landry.

It was the adult Shell who bent over him now. Of that he was certain. As she turned to rummage in the first-aid kit at the foot of the bed, her long hair draped itself across his ankle, producing a tremor of pleasure that approached pain.

She was oblivious to his response, giving her total concentration to taking care of his wound. She deftly strapped tapes across it to pull it closed, her fingers soft on his skin. She was *treating* him, for the love of Mike, not caressing him! What the hell was wrong with him, letting his libido get the upper hand like that? Dammit, where was his control?

She moved again, and the glow of the oil lamp sent golden flames dancing across her impossibly sleek hair. It was so pale, draping down around her face and shoulders in a thick curtain. And straight, dead straight. He remembered it as being golden, yes, but curly—tight, bouncy curls that had circled her laughing, elfin face.

Had he ever touched her hair then? He thought not. Now, though, he wanted very badly to touch it, to see if it felt as silky as it looked. He wanted to speak to her, to see if the slightly tilted light green eyes he recalled would turn to him with eagerness, as they once had. He wanted to discover if the mercurial sprite he remembered from childhood remained within the depths of the woman Shell had become.

He lay still and floated in and out of the past

while she worked on his leg, taping the thick dressing in place.

Summertime, and a little girl named Shirley, who'd called herself Shell. He'd played on a beach with a Shell, and the two of them had giggled about it. Fun. Fairy tales. She had seemed like a character out of a fairy tale to him then, soft and golden, with little freckles all over her like a dusting of sunlight, so different from him with his dark hair and sun-dark skin.

As she continued her ministrations, working on his feet now, dabbing, cleaning, bandaging, he worried about his scars, wishing she didn't have to see them. But there was nothing he could do about it while this drug filled his head with fluff, slowed his thoughts, sent his memories skipping like flat stones on still water.

Big girls hated his scars.

She poured some kind of liquid over a laceration on his foot, and he stiffened, gritting his teeth so as not to make a sound. But his breath drew in sharply despite his good intentions, and she lifted her head, looking directly at him. "I'm sorry," she murmured.

Her eyes were still green, still almond-shaped, but instead of laughter, they held contrition. She didn't like hurting him.

Absurdly, he wanted to comfort her. With great effort and concentration he raised a hand and tucked her hair behind her ear, draping it over her shoulder. It felt as silky as he'd fantasized, but much heavier, richer.

He smiled. "You're a hard lady to track down,"

he said, fighting to enunciate clearly. "Shirley Elizabeth Landry, all growed up."

As he spoke, a loud crash sounded elsewhere in the house, and a shuddering made the entire structure tremble. As if he were somehow responsible, she fixed a horrified gaze on him as her hand went to her mouth to muffle a cry. Then, spinning around, she fled, running toward the source of the noise, the dog scrabbling after her.

Jase tried to heave himself upright, the instinct to *protect* screaming inside him like a siren. The effort was too much as an unseen horse kicked him in the ribs, and he flopped back down, blinding pain stabbing through his chest as darkness flooded into his head.

His last sensation was one of impotent fury at his own weakness before he swirled away into the loud roar of the December storm.

Two

Shell's first, confused thought was to wonder why all those wet, shiny green leaves were plastered against the living-room window. In the next instant she realized that her favorite arbutus tree had fallen, no doubt wiping out her sun deck. Another foot or two to the right, and it would have taken out the bay window, so she supposed she should feel fortunate. She didn't. She felt devastated, as shattered as the trunk of the big, twisted old tree must be.

Her swing! Where would she hang her swing, with the tree gone? It would take a hundred years or more to grow another one that size, and she didn't have a hundred years. She had . . . She had an incipient case of hysteria on her hands, she decided. She also had an unexpected visitor who knew her full name, who remembered her from the past—the past before her tenth year—and whom she couldn't fully place.

What more could go wrong?

The wind whipped up and over the roof. Its pattern changed drastically by the absence of the big old tree, it blew smoke down the chimney, forcing it out around the door of the wood stove and filling the room with an acrid, eye-stinging cloud that set off the smoke detector.

Skeena cowered and put her front legs over her ears, her howls adding to the din. Shell stood on a chair and waved a book catalog at the screaming meemie on her ceiling, clearing the air around it long enough to stop its frantic shrieking.

For a moment she considered pulling out the battery of the device, but good sense prevailed. On a night like this anything, it seemed, could happen, and probably would.

She tiptoed back to the guest room. The man was asleep, apparently undisturbed by all the noise. She quickly bandaged the cut on his foot, covered him completely with the quilt, cleaned up her first-aid supplies, then went to bed.

Once in bed, though, sleep eluded her. She was too aware of the man's presence in her home. What did he want? Why had he blown in with the storm? She'd thought she'd got over distrusting strangers simply because they were strangers. Paranoia, her father often called it. Justifiable reticence, her grandmother insisted, given the kind of childhood she'd suffered. Lil said she'd been painfully shy as a child too.

A sound from the guest room brought her erect, listening, and a moan whipped her out of bed. Still sleeping, the man tossed restlessly, and she wondered if she should waken him and give him more of his medication. The bottle simply said, *Take with food or milk as directed for pain*. What kind of pain was he being treated for? Since he carried pills, it must be something chronic. Had it to do with the scars she'd seen on his legs and torso— deep, puckered purplish and white lines that told of terrible wounds? The scars appeared to be of different ages. What kind of man lived the sort of life where things like that could happen repeatedly to his body?

She wasn't sure she wanted to know. Especially if he had come looking for her, because that meant he was in reality looking for Lilianne.

Lilianne . . . whose dark, intense beauty had captivated the world for that fleeting, scintillating time, beauty that many said would never be equaled. Lilianne . . . that brief, bright flame . . . Like Elvis, like Marilyn, she was "seen" frequently in the oddest places. At a mission in Africa, a convent in France, on a cruise ship in the Caribbean. Too many fans still flatly denied that Lilianne could be dead, especially without a body as proof. So, even after nearly twenty years, the questions were asked in tabloids, on newscasts on the anniversaries of her disappearance, at cocktail parties and on the street—wherever people gathered and gossiped.

Why? How? Where? And sometimes even, ominously, *who?* There were those who believed that, body or not, Lilianne had been murdered by some unknown person who had hidden her away— along with her little daughter, who had also disappeared. But never, not once, had one of those tabloid writers speculated in print that it could have been them and their blood lust for intimate details of a woman's life, their veritable feeding frenzy as they sought what they considered their due, that might have driven her away.

Dread settled over Shell like a wet fog. Had this man come to try to answer those questions? Dammit, where had she seen his face? And since she knew she had, why couldn't she fix it firmly in either time or place?

As if sensing her presence, he opened his eyes, his gaze swinging to her in the doorway.

"Are you feeling a little better?" she asked, picking up the lamp and taking a step closer.

"Yeah." The way he squinted told her it was a lie. He was in pain, but she couldn't let herself care about that. She needed to know who he was; what threat, if any, he presented.

"Who are you?" she asked.

"Don't . . . 'member?"

His words startled her until she realized they were a question, not a statement.

"No, dammit, I don't remember! Tell me your name! Tell me what you want."

"Name's Jase . . . O'Keefe," he said weakly, his words slurred. He licked his lips. "Thirsty. Want . . . drink."

Idiot, that wasn't what I meant, she wanted to shout, but he looked so pathetic, she had to take pity on him. O'Keefe? she thought, as she slipped into the kitchen for a glass of water. That fit the missing letters on his pill bottle, but it didn't turn on any bright illumination in her brain. Returning to the bedroom, she slid a hand under his head and held the glass to his lips. He moaned with pain but managed a sip or two.

"Thanks," he said. It seemed to take a lot of effort for him to force out the word.

"Do you want more pills for pain?"

His eyes rolled crazily as he tried to look at her. "How . . . long?"

"Since you had some? A couple of hours."

"Too . . . soon. More water." He licked his lips again. "So dry."

His bare back felt hot, and she wondered if he was starting a fever. His muscles, hard and sleek, moved under her hand as he shifted, trying to find a more comfortable position. She quickly pulled away, pushing a pillow behind him. He gulped down several long swallows, draining the glass, then closed his eyes, leaning back against the pillows.

"Good," he said with a grateful sigh.

"Would you like more?"

He nodded, not opening his eyes. When she returned with a fresh glass, he was asleep again, his breathing shallow and labored. She set the glass beside him. "Good night," she whispered, neither expecting nor receiving a reply.

"I'm scared," she said to Skeena, who had followed her into the man's room and now padded after her back to her own bedroom. Simply saying it took the edge off the fear, and she slid back under her covers, pulling them up to her chin. The dog turned around several times, then lay down on the mat beside Shell's bed. She sighed once, then began to breathe deeply almost at once, oblivious to the raging storm outside and the weight of worry in her mistress's heart.

"Lucky you," Shell murmured, reaching a hand over the side of the bed to make contact with a familiar, living, breathing creature. She wished she could sleep but knew she wouldn't, not until morning came and she could turn this entire problem over to Ned. As soon as it was even a little bit light, just enough so she could see if a falling tree or branch was aimed at her, she'd get up and go to Ned's house. He'd come back with her and take . . . care of . . . everything. . . .

She was deep in a dream of Lilianne berating a dark-haired photographer who needed a shave, telling him, "You leave Shirl alone! She's only a little girl!," when the horrifying sound of a man's scream jolted her awake.

She knew at once who it was. She flung back the covers and leaped to her feet, groping for the flashlight. With its unsteady beam leading the way, she tore done the hall to where the lamp guttered now, nearly out of fuel and producing evil-smelling black smoke. She blew it out on her way by and flung open the door to O'Keefe's room.

Outside, the storm had dwindled to a faint drizzle, a few halfhearted gusts of wind, and the continued crash of surf on the beach, but inside O'Keefe a greater storm raged. He lay tangled in his bedding, thrashing, his head rolling from side to side as he shouted at someone to get back, to douse that light, to keep down. The sight of his injured leg oozing blood through the bandage was frightening, and she didn't need to touch him to know that his temperature was dangerously high.

If he kept thrashing like that, he'd undo any good she'd done for him.

Aspirin, she thought. That fever had to come down. She darted to the bathroom, got aspirin, rubbing alcohol, and towels, then returned to perch on the side of his bed and force the pills down his throat. He fought her, flailing angrily and muttering dire threats, but swallowed when she told him to, his teeth chattering against the rim of the glass.

While she tried to hold him down, to keep him from hurting himself, he shouted warnings, his voice high and hoarse. She caught his hands and spoke to him in what she hoped was a calming tone, though it wobbled with the fear she couldn't hide from herself. What if he died here with her?

He wouldn't. She wasn't going to let him. Just as she wasn't going to let herself panic. She was an adult and as competent as anybody she knew—with the possible exception of Ned. Lord, but she wished she had some way of getting hold of Ned right this minute.

But she didn't, and she had to deal with this man and his problems herself.

Carefully, mindful of his terrible bruising, she placed one hand on his shoulder to hold him still and began sponging him down with a wet cloth, hoping the evaporating alcohol would cool his burning skin the way it was supposed to. All the while, she spoke in a soothing voice, which seemed to get through to him. He lay quietly as long as she spoke to him, allowing her to work more easily.

When his eyes opened, she thought he was lucid. She smiled and asked, "Feeling better?"

"Oh, yeah," he said gutturally, and clamped hard fingers around the hand resting on his shoulder. "Better than better." Flattening her hand onto his chest, he rubbed it over one of his rocklike nipples. "Feel real good, honey."

Shell jumped. The feel of that nipple under her palm sent an unwelcome shaft of sensation stabbing through her. She snatched her hand away, but he caught it again and clamped it to him. "Don't stop," he said thickly. "Feels . . . great. Cool. So cool. Makes me . . . hot." So quickly that she didn't at first realize what he intended, he dragged her splayed hand down his chest and over his stomach, carrying it directly toward the distinct bulge she could see growing within the confines of his blue briefs.

"Stop that," she said sharply, wresting her hand out of his control and slopping the wet cloth across his mouth and nose. "I'm trying to help you, for heaven's sake." He let go of her hand so he could remove the smothering washcloth.

"You're sick, O'Keefe," she added. And he could take that any way he wanted to.

Suddenly, he laughed, a low, sexy laugh that startled her with its potent ability to charm her. "And you're a prude," he said. His voice was husky, and his eyes glittered challengingly. "Too much of a prude to kiss me?" His tongue passed over his lips with blatant eroticism as he clamped his hands around her back and pulled her closer. "Don't tease, honey," he said cajolingly. "You owe me a kiss."

"I owe you nothing! I'm trying to help you, so just knock it off, buster, or you're on your own here. You can lie in this bed and burn for all I care."

He looked wounded for a moment, like a child who'd been unjustly smacked; then his eyes fell shut again, and his head lolled sideways. His chest heaved with his short, tortured breaths. "I just want . . ." he murmured, but she wasn't to learn what he wanted. His voice trailed away into a shaky sigh, and he appeared to sleep.

She swallowed hard as she continued to fight his fever with the cool sponging. What would it have felt like, under other circumstances, to have responded to his request, to have leaned against him, covered his sculpted lips with her own, and tasted him? For Pete's sake! she told herself. You're as sick as he is!

Still, she couldn't keep her gaze from straying to his hard mouth, his determined chin. A vertical two-inch scar, no wider than a fine-tip pen mark, bisected one cheek, giving him a piratical air. His overlong black hair had not a trace of gray in it, and fell across a broad brow. Deep grooves that she recognized as having more to do with suffering than with age had been carved between his mouth and nose.

The depth and wistfulness of her sigh surprised her.

As if he had heard it, he opened his eyes again, glaring now with irritation. "Jeeze, woman, shut the damned window!" His teeth chattered as he wrapped his arms around himself. "It's colder than a whore's heart in here!"

"Such a colorful vocabulary," she said, toweling him dry, rubbing briskly over his arms and shoulders before drawing the quilt up to his chin. She hadn't meant to freeze him, merely to cool his fever. It appeared, though, she thought with relief, that she'd also cooled his ardor.

Or had she?

He tossed the quilt back. "Come to bed, honey," he said, startling her again with the clarity of his gaze as it locked itself on her eyes. A suggestive smile played seductively over his lips. He patted the mattress. "Let's keep each other warm."

Firmly, Shell tucked the covers back around him. "No. Go to sleep."

His fingers clamped around her wrist. "Don't leave me." Once more, he was that intriguing blend of little boy and tough guy. At least it wasn't difficult to twist her arm free.

"I'll stay until you're asleep." Because, she told herself, he might talk in his sleep and say something that would reveal who he was and what he wanted. She'd stay for that reason and that reason only.

"Closer," he said.

She sat on the side of the bed near his knees. "This is close enough."

"Not nearly."

She gasped in surprise as his arms whipped out from under the quilt, shoving it back, and snaked around her, capturing her and pulling her up over his chest. In spite of the shivering, his skin burned against her. She gently extricated herself from his embrace, holding him down with one hand in the middle of his chest. He glared at her impotently for several moments before sighing and closing his eyes again.

After a couple of minutes Shell thought he was deeply enough asleep for her to leave. She'd just begun easing herself off the side of his bed when he flung himself erect.

His shout, "Carson!" as much as his galvanic jerking upright, frightened her half to death. She tried to push him down, but he was too strong for her now. His eyes were wide, glittering like wet black stones. He looked determined. He also looked demented. "Carson, cover me, I'm going in!"

"Take it easy," Shell said, trying to pin his shoulders. "Jason, don't fight me, please. Lie down. You have to rest because you're ill. I'm trying to help you."

He groaned long and low and despairingly, look-ing straight into her eyes with such loathing, she felt chilled. "You? You never helped me," he said bitterly. "You left me!" He choked, squeezed his eyes shut for a moment, then opened them and stared at her. He clamped one hand onto the back of her head, fingers tangling in her hair. "Oh, God, baby, why?" he asked. "Why did you go?"

"Jason, lie down. Please. Try to relax."

"Ahh, get the hell out of here," he said, thrusting her away. "I don't want you back."

"Okay, that's fine. Just lie down and let me cover you."

Abruptly, his look of hatred was gone, replaced by one of pleading, of endless, depthless yearning that closed Shell's throat with pain. He caught her by the elbows and held her before him, his voice low and grating as he said, "I don't want you to go, Mai-Lee. But . . . how could I ever again trust you to stay with me? Could I ever believe in you again after what you did? You have to understand, baby. It can never be the same again for us, so go. Please, by all that's merciful, get out, before I let the loneliness take over and beg you to come back. . . ."

His eyes closed. He fell silent, but didn't let her go. Shell sat very still, waiting for his hands to relax in sleep, but abruptly his eyes popped open again. "Why, Mai-Lee?" His exhalation was short and abrupt, like a sob. "Please! Mai-Lee, I wanted you for so long. . . . I waited and waited, and you never came back, so if you leave me now, I'll . . ." His voice trailed away as he gazed at her, those coal-black eyes boring into hers, searching for answers that weren't hers to give.

He cupped her face then, drew her down to him, and took from her a kiss that also was not hers to give. Her head pressed to his chest, he rested his palm on her cheek. His fingers slid through her hair, tenderly, seductively, as if the feel of it so pleasured him, he couldn't stop moving his skin against it.

"Soft," he murmured against her temple. "So soft."

His head fell back onto the pillows while he continued to hold her. He stroked her cheek, his fingertips hard, callused, sending shivers of forbidden delight down her throat and chest to gather at and pucker her nipples. Her other cheek lay on the powerful muscles of his chest, and she drew in a long breath of his scent. He smelled clean and masculine, and the sound of his heart pounding steadily in her ear was as soothing as the feel of him, the scent of him, were disturbing.

With a strength that amazed her, he suddenly lifted her fully onto the bed, rolling up and over her and pinning her to the mattress with his weight. Cupping her face in one hand, he kissed her again, this time demanding a response. Even as she fought not to give it, she succumbed to all the wild sensations that refused her denial.

As Shell told herself that this was wrong, crazy, that Jason O'Keefe was a stranger who was sick with a fever and out of his mind, her heart told her that she had known him from the beginning of time and that this was as right as anything she had ever experienced.

The heat of his fever burned her skin, and a different kind of heat grew within her, one that was all hers and building inexorably, glowing hotter and hotter. She tried to drag herself away before she got lost in the sensations of his smooth, hot tongue prodding her lips, before she gave way to the demands of his mouth. But needs she had suppressed for too long arose and weakened her, gave her muscles all the effectiveness of old rubber bands and melted her inner resolve. She slid an arm around his neck, touching his hair with uncertain fingers. Its springy thickness was a delight, and she filled her hand with it.

The hard plunge of his tongue softened, and he coaxed and beguiled as heat built deep within her. She shuddered as his tongue flicked and teased, and his hands stroked over her, one gliding down her back to her waist, the other cradling her head as he held her securely. His hand trailed out of her hair, across her shoulder, and down to cup a breast, sending a shaft of desire straight through her.

In response to her involuntary surge against him, he moaned, deepened the kiss, and then, almost as if he'd accomplished what he'd set out to do, he stopped. He eased his hold on her and let his lips trail over her cheek and down her neck. He slipped sideways, his head falling back onto the pillows. *Asleep!*

Or passed out.

Shell drew in a shuddering breath and somewhere found the strength to slide out from under his pinning weight. She sat on the floor beside the bed, clutching her arms around her middle and trying to catch her breath.

"Shell," he murmured, a limp hand draping over her hair. "Little Shell. Don't go."

Shakily, she got to her knees and stared at him. What had he said?

His eyes were closed. A soft snore arose from him. His skin, when she touched his shoulder, was cooler. He seemed calmer now, sleeping easily, no longer beset by nightmares.

Inside her chest, though, her heart beat as rapidly as if she were running for her very life. At what point during that embrace had she ceased to be Mai-Lee to him and become Shell?

Presently, feeling chilled and even more frightened, she slipped out of his room and back to her own bed, completely forgetting her notion of staying there in case he said something revealing in his sleep. Oh, Lord, who was Jason O'Keefe? What did he want from her?

Whatever it was, especially if it was information, he wouldn't get it, she vowed, punching her pillow into shape. With Ned's help she would make sure of that. She must.

In the morning, she promised herself, she'd get the man out of her house and off Piney Point, if she had to piggyback him all the way to town. She'd be happier still when he was completely off the Sunshine Coast and back in California.

She dozed fitfully for a couple of hours and awakened to watch the world turn gray. Tiptoeing to the door of O'Keefe's room, she saw he still slept soundly, his chest rising and falling evenly.

Soon, after dressing warmly for work in dark slacks and a red sweater, she had the fire burning brightly in the living-room wood stove. Working quickly and quietly, she readied the old-fashioned percolator she used at times like these and set it on top of the warm stove.

After shoving her feet into black boots, she grabbed a jacket and let Skeena out for an early morning run on the beach. Following the dog, she rounded the house to the front and mourned the loss of her arbutus tree far more than she mourned the loss of the porch.

The ocean still ran high, swells creaming and frothing as they struck the shore of a distant islet, then booming with earthshaking thunder as they hammered in close to where she strode. But the sky was clear, the breeze mild.

The dog raced happily after a crow that teased it unmercifully by keeping always one short hop ahead. Shell smiled and told herself that her nighttime fears had been simply that, nighttime fears that the day had washed away. How could she be troubled when navy-blue water trimmed with white lace stretched all the way to where Vancouver Island, twenty-five miles to the west, thrust its white-capped peaks into the blue winter sky? Thin streamers of cloud streaked along above, catching the rays of the sun and making the entire world sparkle.

Jason O'Keefe was no danger to her, or to her mother, or to their peace of mind. Even as the thought crossed her mind, she remembered his kiss. Shivering, she wrapped her arms around herself and whistled for Skeena to come back. That kiss, the one that might have been meant for another woman but also might have been meant for her, told her that he, whoever he was, could very well be a danger to her. The sooner she got him on his feet and on his way, the better off she'd be.

The first step in that maneuver would be a big cup of strong, hot coffee to sharpen her wits, give her courage, and set her up for the day.

Surely, it would be perked by now.

Three

Shell had just walked back inside when she heard O'Keefe stumble from his room to the bathroom. By the time he emerged, she had her coffee poured and was reaching up to get a cup down for him. Hearing his soft, bare footfalls on the tile behind her, she forced herself to look over her shoulder and meet his gaze, and wondered if he could hear the loud hammering of her heart.

She swept her gaze over him, the broad shoulders, muscular arms, and bruised chest visible above the green blanket wrapped high around his body. It parted as he took a halting step into the room, revealing the bandage she'd put on the night before. Blood had soaked through.

"You're a real mess," she said. "I don't know how you managed to get here, the shape you're in."

He grinned a totally irresistible grin that made something very elemental flip over inside her.

"Hell, honey," he drawled. "A man's gotta do what a man's gotta do."

Shell had to laugh. "I see. You're just a natural-born hero, are you?"

He nodded, looking comically smug. "Just wait till you're in peril, Pauline. I'll show you what a big, strong hero I am."

Abruptly, she was all tangled up in the memory of his strong arms holding her, of that hot kiss in the dark night. Warmth stung her cheeks as she wondered if he had any recollection of it.

Again, she swept her gaze over his blanket-wrapped shape, swallowing hard at the sight of his sleep-tousled hair and the full day's growth of beard on his face. Her skin tingled as she remembered the feel of that beard. He was handsome, virile, and disturbing on more than one front. She was going to have to stay on her guard, not let him see that he scared her. Vultures and sharks attacked the vulnerable; the only protection was strength.

"Go back to bed," she said briskly, pouring coffee from the heavy percolator. "I'll bring your coffee to your room, where you'll be warmer: It's still too cold out here for you. What do you take in it?"

Instead of obeying, he limped the rest of the way into the kitchen and pulled out a wooden chair. "Both," he said, sinking onto it. He winced, sticking his sore leg out before him as if unable to bend it.

She set his cup on the table, along with powdered creamer and sugar. "You shouldn't be up," she said but dragged another chair closer and lifted his foot onto it.

She poured him a glass of apple juice and set it beside his coffee. "How's the pain?" she asked, picking up his pill bottle.

His gesture indicated he didn't want any. "It's not too bad." He took a healthy gulp of the juice. "They're for migraine, but they seem to have worked on the rest of the agony too. Apart from a few dull aches, I feel pretty well human."

"That's good," she said. "Now, suppose you—" *tell me who you are and what you want,* she had been about to say, but he let the blanket slide down several inches, and she broke off, gasping as even worse purple bruising was revealed.

He prodded experimentally with blunt fingertips. "Nothing's broken. I'm pretty sure of that."

"How can you be?" He'd looked bad enough the night before. Today he looked as if he'd been sent through a log peeler. "I'd still like to have a doctor look you over. If you feel up to traveling by car, I'll take you into town with me when I go to work and drop you off at the emergency room. Otherwise, I'll have to send an ambulance for you."

His black eyebrows drew together. "I don't need a doctor, and I'm not going to any emergency room. Besides, unless there's another road out onto this point, I'm not going anywhere and neither are you. The road I came in on is washed out. That's what happened to me. I drove smack into a river as I came around a bend and had to fight my way out of the wreck of my Jeep."

"River?" Shell frowned and bit her lip. She remembered he'd said something about a washout, and he had arrived soaking wet, and yes, the creek could turn into a river during a deluge. "That must mean the bridge is out. Damn! We lost it a few years ago in another storm, and it took them nearly a week to get it replaced."

She paced to the front window where the wet leaves still pressed against the glass, then back toward Jason O'Keefe. She picked up the phone, but there was still no dial tone. She slammed it down. "Dammit, I have to get to work!"

"I'm sorry," he said, as if somehow the washout had been his fault. "Are you a nurse?"

She blinked in surprise. "No. I own a bookstore."

For an instant she thought she saw a flicker of wariness in his eyes. "Oh." He shoved the edge of the blanket back from his leg and looked down at the dressing. "I wondered." He glanced up, and whatever she had seen was gone, leaving his expression bland. "You did a pretty good job on me last night."

"I . . . took a home-nursing course once," she said, frowning at the blood-soaked bandage. Surely, it needed to be changed if infection was to be avoided. And it was, at all costs, because she wanted this man mobile enough to ford the stream when it went down, and to hike the mile and a half to the highway so he could hitch a ride into town. Whatever his reason for being on Piney Point, she didn't want him to tarry.

Collecting her first-aid kit, she set it on the table, then strode to the sink to wash her hands. They trembled under the stream of lukewarm water, which was all the water heater was providing that morning.

What was the matter with her? she asked herself. She was simply going to change his dressing, the same one she'd put on his thigh the night before. That was nothing to get agitated over, was it? But . . . he'd kissed her, held her, stroked his big hands over her, and somehow that changed everything, made the mere idea of touching him a threat to her equilibrium.

Squaring her shoulders, she dried her hands on a clean towel and lectured herself. Okay, so he'd kissed her, and held her, and caressed her, and she'd responded much too readily. But that had been last night. Today things would be different. She had only to make it so.

Yet her fingers still trembled.

Jase watched Shell, smiling as he recalled the small, earnest face of the child who had said to him, "My name's not really Shell. It's Shirley Elizabeth Landry, but I can't say that, so I say Shell." He'd laughed at her then, and laughed with her many times. When their summer together was over, he'd let her fade from his memory, not remembering her until he'd come across an old photograph with her name written on the back.

Now he admired the way she'd grown up. He liked the fit of her slacks over her nicely rounded rump, the way they tightened around her shapely thighs as she walked. Still, his mind searched for remnants of the girl he had known, for Shell Landry the adult was not what he'd expected, despite the grainy newspaper picture he'd seen a couple of weeks ago. Tall and slim, with the same pale green eyes he remembered, she exuded confidence one moment and looked frail and vulnerable the next. She couldn't be called pretty. Her features were too strong for that, too much personality showed through, but she was most assuredly attractive. Her scarlet sweater gave her skin a lovely glow, and her stunning pale hair was tied carelessly at her nape with a paisley scarf.

She came back toward him, drying her hands on a towel and not looking at him. She seemed to be pretending he didn't exist as a person, even when she crouched before him and placed one hand on his knee to steady herself.

He dumped half a teaspoonful of sugar onto the table as his body reacted to her touch with shocking swiftness. Drawing in a deep breath, he recalled the same swift response to her in the night, and suddenly he remembered kissing her, holding her pinned against his chest, rolling her under him and wanting her so badly, he'd thought he'd die if he couldn't have her. He remembered her lips parting, her tongue seeking his, at first shyly, then with a boldness that heated his blood as he relived it. Lord, she'd been soft . . . her skin, her breasts, her hair, even the scent of her had been soft . . . and sweet and—

"I'll do this quick," she said, and at the same moment snatched up the tape, pulling out leg hairs by the roots.

"Damn!" he gasped, but at least the sharp sting had taken care of his erotic response to her touch. It wouldn't continue to, though, if she kept touching his leg. He groaned softly, eliciting a murmured apology from her as she gently examined the edges of his wound and the flesh surrounding it.

"You heal quickly," she said, her head still down. He wished she'd look at him, wished she'd remove those long, slender, trembling fingers from his leg before the blanket over his lap could no longer hide his reaction.

"Maybe your kiss made it better," he said before he could bite back the words.

"What?" Her head jerked up, and she stared at him, her eyes full of disconcertion, anger, and . . . was it shame? Why should she be ashamed of kissing him? Unless . . . was she involved with someone else? "I thought you were too delirious to remember that," she said in a thin voice as she bent her head again.

"I don't forget when someone like you kisses me."

She flared beautifully. "I didn't kiss you, O'Keefe. You kissed me." She slapped the new dressing in place, briskly sticking down the tape. Dragging the blanket back over him, she added, "Or more accurately, I'd have to say you kissed someone named Mai-Lee. At any rate, you had no right to do it. If you hadn't been injured and burning up with fever, I'd have clocked you a good one."

He clamped a hand around her wrist. Mai-Lee? He'd talked about Mai-Lee? He must have been raving! "Mai-Lee lies a long way back in my past," he said. In an attempt to distract her from that subject, he went on. "Not as far back as you do, though. And if I kissed her instead of you in my delirium, I'd better remedy that. Every woman deserves to be kissed for her own sake."

Besides, he thought, looking at her snapping green eyes, her flushed cheeks, and her taut body, crouched as if she were about to spring up and flee, he wanted to kiss Shell Landry again, and not for old times' sake.

"Just who the hell are you, O'Keefe?" Her hostility whipped him as she jumped to her feet and tried to twist her wrist free. "What have you come here for? What do you want?"

"Want?" he said, drawing her between his legs and snaking an arm around her waist. "I want to get to know you again." He tugged her down until she half sprawled across his uninjured leg. Her one hand was braced behind him on the back of the chair, the other on his shoulder, and her eyes were wide and startled. "As to what I've come for, Shell," he added, realizing something that hadn't occurred to him until that moment, "I've come to stake a claim."

And then he staked it.

Shock held Shell immobile for the first few seconds. Then something else did. His firm lips parted hers with forthright determination, and sighing, she opened for the thrust of his tongue, welcoming it, accepting it, accepting him, not knowing why she did, only that she must. He tasted of apple juice and coffee—and man.

Unlike the kiss of the previous night, Shell knew from the outset, and not just because he'd said so, that this one was all for her. He was doing exactly what he'd said, staking a claim, but what claim? And why on her?

She wanted to demand answers, wanted to struggle, but her mind whirled in a chaotic medley of thought and emotion that left her reeling, needing to cling to something solid. The only solid object at hand, though, was him.

As his hold gentled, becoming almost unbearably tender, her unease was swept away by an uncanny sense of rightness, a feeling that she should melt into him, lean against his firm chest. She wanted to nestle close, closer, offer more of herself, because he seemed to be giving all of himself through the heat of his lips, the gentleness of his touch, the strength of his arms.

He cradled her face with one hand, fingers stroking down under her chin and across her throat in a caress she was utterly unable to resist. It sent a singing joy through her blood, and a heavy, hot pulsing along her nerve endings that centered in the very core of her, making her want—and making her wanton. As if he knew that, he slowed the caress, putting even more sensuality into it. He curved his entire palm around the front of her throat, his fingers sliding up under her hair, his thumb making small circles below her ear as a low, intense hum of appreciation emanated from him.

Had anyone ever touched her like that, with an innate certainty that it was the right caress for her, as if it were designed with Shell Landry, her needs and desires, in mind? And how did he know what was exactly right for her, when she wasn't even sure she knew herself? Had that specific touch always been the one that would arouse her faster and deeper than any other? She couldn't remember, didn't want to think. She wanted only to have his fingers go on and on, stroking over her skin in exactly that way. She wanted this kiss never to end, but to taste him, feel him, breathe in his scent, forever.

The scent of him made her dizzy, tempted her to breathe deeper and deeper to capture it all. It was faintly like lime, or was it leather? Or perhaps some exotic, foreign spice? The flexing of the powerful muscles of his arm, the hardness of his thigh under her hips, urged her to dissolve into his embrace, to become one with him.

Something compelled her to stroke his skin, to know him as he knew her, and she lifted a hand to his face. She rubbed the raspy stubble on his jaw, traced the shape of his nose, the straight line of an eyebrow, the curve of an ear, then slid her hand down to his neck, finding a wild, powerful pulse there. She glided her palm across his chest as she had the night before, but this time she did it all for herself. Not to cool him, not even to heat him, though his erect nipple and ragged breathing told her she was doing that. The need to feel his body against her hand was paramount, so she stroked, taking and receiving something good, something special, something that she knew deep inside she deserved.

It was he who broke the kiss, slowly, reluctantly, pulling his head back from her. His eyes, dazed now, stared into hers.

"Oh, brother!" he said softly, but with an emphasis she could fully understand. His smile was full of wonder, awe, and not inconsiderable confusion.

She nodded and stood, seeking a chair on the far side of the table before her legs collapsed under her. Never taking her eyes off him, she simply sat there, wondering what had come over her.

Neither spoke until Skeena scratched eagerly at the back door. Shell leaned over and opened it, letting in the wet animal. Skeena licked her hand, then stood stiff-legged and wary, staring at Jason O'Keefe. Finally, perhaps sensing that Shell was in no danger, she went to her food and water dishes and began eating.

Dragging herself out of her befuddlement, Shell ran the tip of her tongue over her lips. It felt completely different from his tongue, but the taste of him was still there, making her insides quiver. She clamped her arms one over the other, hands clutching her elbows. Her crossed arms almost contained the shivers that continued to ripple through her as she relived the sensations that kiss had aroused. Almost.

Dammit, what was the matter with her? she asked herself yet again. Her acceding to that kiss had probably given the man far too many wrong impressions of her. Now that a good, sturdy table separated her from him, she'd better start reeducating him. To say nothing of her own heart, which still thudded much too rapidly. She had to breathe deeply several times before she could speak, injecting a hint of acid into her tone.

"I guess," she said, "it hasn't cropped up recently in conversation in California, maybe because it's been known for so long by so many, but caveman tactics are considered passé."

She tried to decide if there had been a tinge of regret in her voice for the passing of caves and cavemen. She hoped not.

He grinned unrepentantly. "It can hardly be considered a caveman tactic to take what I was promised a long, long time ago."

She tilted her chin higher. "Promised? By whom?"

"By you, darlin'. One warm summer afternoon."

"What?"

He smiled. It was a nice smile. A bit crooked, it creased the skin bracketing his mouth and filled his eyes with dancing lights. It was far and away the most disarming smile she had ever seen, and she was hard put not to return it.

"*I* promised *you* a kiss? When?"

"Well, it was a while back," he confessed ruefully. "So I guess I can't blame you for having forgotten. You said, 'When we're all grown up, we'll get married, and you can kiss me, and we'll have lots of babies.'" He grinned again, then leaned across the table and touched her face, drawing his fingertips from her temple to her chin and down her throat, leaving her tense and shivering outwardly and all loose and warm inside. She was not sure it was a feeling she liked, but on the other hand, she didn't think she wanted it to stop, either. "But I do remember," he said, "so can you blame me for collecting?"

She said nothing, waiting for him to continue. It was completely out of her range now. He was spouting a lot of garbage. She hoped. *When* could she have met him before? In another life? She would remember a man like this. Forever. Even through the veils of other lives.

"I can only hope," he went on, "that that kiss didn't have such a drastic effect. As you may have noticed, we aren't married."

"Yes." She drew an unsteady breath and forced her tone to impart tartness. "You should be careful with your kisses, if they have that result."

"Honey, I'm always careful. And you must be, too, since you're close to thirty and I don't see any of those babies crawling around the floor."

"How could you possibly know my age?"

"By extrapolation."

She looked at him questioningly, and he explained. "By deducting three-and-a-half years from my own age. You were that much younger than me when you made me that promise, so I assume you still are. Unless you're one of those women who stops having birthdays at twenty-five?"

"Not me," she said. "I enjoy birthday gifts too much to do that."

He laughed. "Good for you." He touched her face again. "I'll have to remember that."

Shell jerked away. "All right, when did I make such a rash promise to a man I don't even remember? And why?"

"When? More than twenty-three years ago. Why? Because you'd just eaten a mouthful of baby crabs, and I fed you the last of my candy to make you feel better."

She stared at him as memories swirled around in her mind, solidified, clarified, brightened. "Jase?"

she whispered, as if tasting the word. "Jase . . . Not Jason but . . . *Jase*. Of course! I should have remembered! But . . . O'Keefe doesn't ring any kind of bell."

"Maybe you never knew my last name."

"Maybe. Good grief . . . such a long time ago. Sand castles, chocolate-covered raisins, and—" She gulped. "Crabs." She shuddered with remembered disgust. "Oh, yuck!"

Gazing at each other, they shared a moment's laughter, warm and friendly, connected by a vivid image dredged up out of the past.

Jase's heart did strange things as Shell's laughter rose in an irrepressible tide, bubbling out of her as she stared at him in mingled delight and disbelief. She smiled as her laughter died, a big, wide, all-over-her-face smile that lit up her eyes and crinkled her nose, and Jason O'Keefe came closer to falling in love than he ever had before.

That day, Shell remembered, she'd sat on the beach in her yellow bathing suit—it had had frills around the rump and across the top, and strings that tied behind her neck—and built a castle with Jase on a little patch of sand in front of a cottage very similar to the one they sat in now. Lord! A whole continent away. A whole lifetime ago. A summer of magic and joy and castles in the sand.

Castles, of course, had needed occupants, and the tiny crabs, no bigger than a child's thumbnail, that lived under the rocks at the edge of the sandspit were available. Jase had been sharing his chocolate-coated raisins with her, and she, off in a dream with one hand full of raisins and the other full of crabs, had momentarily forgotten which hand was which . . .

"After you'd spit out the crabs," Jase reminded her, "and washed out your mouth and finished all my raisins to 'take the taste away,' you told me you loved me best of all and that when we were big, we'd get married, and I could kiss you, and then we'd have lots of babies."

She looked at him in wonder. "I was six and a half."

He nodded. "And I was ten." They gazed at each other, and Shell could almost feel the heat of the summer sun. She remembered the long days of play, the feel of the sand, the scent of salt and driftwood and smoke from beach fires along the Rhode Island shore. She closed her eyes to savor the memories, recalling, too, the taste of ripe, juicy peaches, the slow, flooding sweetness of strawberries crushed against the roof of her mouth, the delight of chocolate-covered raisins—and having a friend for the very first time in her life.

Of course there had been other friends since, other summers and other treats, but that summer had been special, not only because of having a friend. It had given her the one thing she had never enjoyed before—total privacy and her mother all to herself. No one had known who she was, or more important, who her mother was.

There had been no huge Hollywood house with its servants and security, no on-location trailer. There had been no governess, no big car with its driver who took her mother away every morning before Shell awoke and sometimes didn't return her until after Shell was in bed. There had been no cameras, no flashbulbs dazzling her eyes, no prying questions or gushy reporters wanting to touch her hair or fluff out her dress or admire her and ask her if she wanted to grow up to be exactly like her beautiful mama.

She opened her eyes and found Jase still gazing at her. She forced a smile. Inside, a clamoring voice asked if he remembered her mother, too, and if he had, as he matured, become aware of exactly who it was he remembered? And if so, what did he intend to do with the knowledge?

Panic rippled through her as she searched his face. She found nothing there to say her fears were rational, but nothing, either, to say they weren't. Oh, Lord help her—even if he hadn't yet realized the significance of his recalling that summer, he might in time, and then what? Could he be trusted?

How strange that he was the first person to come out of her childhood like this. How protected she—they—had been the past twenty years, how secure they'd become, thinking they had only to guard against the obvious dangers. And now, because one man remembered a summertime friend from long ago, was all the fine security they'd built in danger of coming apart?

"Imagine," she said, "your remembering me and my crabs all these years."

"Imagine my remembering your saying you'd marry me." His dark eyes danced. "Of course, that was the first time a woman ever proposed marriage to me. I guess that's not something a guy forgets."

"How many women have proposed marriage to you since?"

He shrugged. "Not so very many."

He looked away, and the name Mai-Lee suddenly hung between them like a piece of soiled laundry, ruining the mood of camaraderie they'd been building with their memories. Had Mai-Lee proposed marriage to him? Shell wondered. Had he proposed marriage to her? Why had Mai-Lee left, and if she ever came back, would Jason O'Keefe reach out to her as he had the night before, clinging to her as if he'd hold her forever? And, dammit, what did it matter?

"You know," she said, breaking the uncomfortable silence, "it's funny, but when you first arrived last night, I thought there was something familiar about you. It drove me crazy, especially once I knew your name and still couldn't make the link between a vaguely familiar face and the reality of a man named Jason O'Keefe. How could we have been such good friends and known so little about each other—such as last names?"

"I knew yours, but maybe you never needed to know mine because we were kids, and children are very accepting of one another. They don't require details. For instance, I had no idea that summer that I was playing with a little heiress."

Though his face became slyly thoughtful, his eyes laughed secretly as he said, "Hmm, now that I think of it, maybe I should demand my rights as your affianced husband. After all, if you refuse, it could be considered breach of promise. Might be worth a great deal."

Her jaw tensed. "I'd say that no court in the land

would expect me to uphold a promise I'd made before I was old enough to cross the street alone."

He laughed. "Yeah. Worse luck." He waggled his brows. "Damn. I've never tried blackmail as a means of courting a lady."

She relaxed. He might think of her as an heiress, but she sensed he wasn't after money. "No? Why, you poor, deprived man." As if poking a sore tooth, she added, "We'll have to find you one with something to hide."

Her words elicited not a glimmer of secret knowledge on his face, or guilt, or even a spark of suspicion that maybe she *could* have something to hide. Either he was a superb actor or he truly did suspect nothing about her mother's identity.

Shell breathed much easier. It really was all right, she told herself. Leaning forward, she folded her arms on the table. "So, tell me where you've been since we were children. What kinds of exciting things have you done? You wanted to be an explorer, if I remember correctly. Tell me about your life."

He shrugged. "I've been lots of places, done lots of things, though I was more what you'd call an adventurer than an explorer. Still, it's been an . . . interesting life, so far."

"Earning scars," she said quietly, not asking but letting him know she'd like to understand why and how he had them, if he wanted to share that information.

He met her gaze steadily. "That too," he said, declining to go into detail about them. "But no more. Now I spend my life—"

He broke off as the dog leaped to her feet.

Barking loudly, she flung herself at the back door even before it was swept open and a red-faced man burst through. He was dripping from the waist down. As Jase watched, his hackles suddenly up and stiff, the other man strode in and swept Shell—who had jumped to her feet with the same alacrity as the dog—into a bear hug.

"Shell!" the man exclaimed. "Wasn't that a terrible night? I'm sorry I couldn't get back. Are you all right?"

Four

Jase sat rigid, struggling not to leap up and pop the man a good one right between the eyes. What the hell was the matter with him? He had no right to object. Still, he didn't mind a bit when Shell wriggled out of that embrace.

"Ned, I'm all right," she said. "What do you mean, you couldn't get back? Were you away?"

"Yes," he said, jamming a hand through his hair and dislodging a confetti storm of sawdust. "Nola and I went into Sechelt last night to have dinner with her sister. We couldn't get back because of all the trees across the road."

"Across the road?" Shell laughed. "Have you seen my front deck?"

"I saw. And the crick's washed out too. There's a Jeep with California plates"—Ned's tone became scathing—"ass-end up right in the middle of it, and . . ." As Shell stepped aside, Ned appeared to have noticed Jase for the first time. "Oh. Yours, huh?"

Holding the blanket around himself, Jase stood and limped to Shell's side. He put a hand on her shoulder in a foolishly proprietary gesture. It pleased him to note that he was nearly a head taller than the other man. "Mine," he said, not even trying to put any friendliness into his voice. He caught the look of startled surprise Shell bounced between him and the man she'd called Ned.

Shell bit her lip, not knowing whether to laugh, cry, or get mad. What the hell was going on here? On Ned's part, of course, he was responding to those California license plates, but what could account for Jase's prickly behavior? That icy stare should have frozen Ned's wet pants right to his frame.

"Jase," she said, "this is Ned Mason, my next-door neighbor. Ned, meet Jason O'Keefe, an old friend from long ago."

Ned glared. "Yeah?"

"Yeah," Jase said, and Shell almost expected him to add, *Wanna make somethin' of it?*

Quickly, she said, "Ned, you're soaked! What happened to you?"

"Told you. Crick's washed out half the road. I discovered that on my way home this morning. As soon as it was daylight, I got a chain saw and started cutting my way through. There were nineteen trees down in the mile and a half between the crick and the highway. That's why it took me so long to get here."

He scowled from her to Jase and back. "Did you think I'd abandoned you?"

"Oh, Ned, of course not. Nineteen trees? You must be worn out. Come sit down and have some coffee. And how about something to eat?"

"Uh-uh." Ned shook his head. "Nola and Grace made sure I got fed before I left the village this morning, and I've still got too much to do outside. The arbutus isn't the only tree we lost out here by the beach. There's a couple down between here and your—" He cast a suspicious glance at Jase, who had gone back to his chair and had his foot propped up again. "Between here and Ms. Harris's place," he went on, "and I want to get them out."

Shell glanced at her watch. "Mom won't even be up yet," she said, and grinned. "Don't go using a power saw over by their house, or you'll have Maureen outside throwing rocks at you."

Ned shrugged and looked at his own watch. "Yeah. I guess you're right. I've been out of bed so long, it feels like noon already." He cast another look at Jase and his blanket, his sleep-tousled hair.

"I managed to hook a bag and another case out of the back of that Jeep. Want 'em?"

Jase's face lit up. "They're here?"

Ned opened the door and tossed inside a soggy-looking, battered leather tote; then, with more respect, handed Shell a laptop computer. Behind her, Jase breathed out a long sigh of relief. He took the computer from her and set it on the table, wiping its case dry with one corner of his blanket.

"Thank you," he said, nodding at the other man, but Ned had already turned away from him.

"I told Nola to call What's-er-name," he was saying to Shell, "that assistant of yours, and let her know you were stranded out here. I guess she can run the store okay for you."

"Of course she can. Ned, thanks." Again, Shell hugged him.

"Not very friendly, is he?" Jase asked after Ned had left. "At least toward other men. He seemed pretty pally with you."

Shell heard the hard tension in his voice and stared at him in disbelief. "I've known Ned Mason since I was ten years old. He and his wife work for my mother's friend, Maureen. He's a handyman, a gardener, a general fixer-upper, and is invaluable besides being a damned good friend. Nola, his wife, is my mother and Maureen's housekeeper. He looks upon himself as sort of an honorary uncle to me, I think."

Jase felt chastened. "Oh. Well, okay."

"Okay?" Shell planted her fists on her hips. "What do you mean, 'okay'? Are you giving me *permission* to hug Ned?"

He bit his lip, feeling more than just mildly uncomfortable under her furious glare. Hell, yes, he realized, that was exactly what he'd been doing, and it was crazy, as crazy as his reaction to seeing her in another man's arms had been. He was having a testosterone fit. That's what his sister Jenny called what had just inexplicably happened to him. He'd heard her use the term with an affectionate, derisive laugh, poking her husband in his slight paunch when she said it. His brother-in-law was the jealous type.

Jase, absolutely, was not. It was simply that

Shell's eagerness to greet the other man had startled him, especially in light of the way she'd responded to his kiss only minutes before. He had not been jealous.

"No, of course I'm not giving you permission," he said. "Sorry about that. Must have been some kind of atavistic instinct brought on by this time warp we're in. A weird kind of need to protect an old girlfriend."

Shell's nostrils flared. "Time warp?"

Damn, he'd offended her again. "That's what I thought in the night. You in that long gown with ruffles around the throat, the oil lamps, the rocking chair with its patchwork cushions. It was as if I'd traveled back a hundred years." He smiled. "It was kind of a nice feeling."

As he said it, he knew it was true. He, who had sworn, after too many tours of duty in too many primitive places, never to live again without the amenities, had felt a strange affinity for Shell Landry's particular time warp. "But obviously," he went on, "it made me act as if I were living a hundred years in the past."

Shell's anger abated with his apology, and she refilled their coffee mugs before sitting down. "Maybe you better stay out of time warps, then, if that's what they do to you."

Laughter lit up his eyes. "How else can I find old girlfriends if I don't employ time travel?"

"You do a lot of it?" She grinned. "Isn't it sort of dangerous, looking them up? Is that where you got all those scars?"

The question was a definite challenge, but Jase refused to answer it. He'd rather not have her know what he had done to earn those scars. And oddly enough, he realized that as long as he remained trapped in her time warp, he'd rather not have her know what he did now. Too many people, men and women alike, wanted to be friends with someone they saw as having a little bit of fame. It would be nice, he thought, if Shell could be his friend again simply because she liked him.

But . . . it was dumb to go looking for friendship in a place where he had no intention of lingering, wasn't it? He glanced out the window beside him. It revealed a sweep of grass littered with broken evergreen boughs and twigs, a wall of tangled brush, and a sliver of bright blue ocean with lacy whitecaps on it.

It was the first time in more than five years he had looked out a window and not seen another building, and he wasn't sure he liked the feeling of isolation it gave him.

Isolation, the loneliness it bred. That was what was really dangerous. It led a man to do foolish, ill-considered things.

Realizing she was still waiting for an answer about his scars, he glanced back at her. "I could have gotten them from old girlfriends. Old girlfriends can be dangerous."

After a moment she said, "I'm waiting to learn why you looked up this 'old girlfriend,' Jase, and why you suddenly remembered me and went to the trouble of seeking me out after more than twenty years."

He sighed. "Are you going to be offended when I confess that I didn't really remember you? That for a long time I'd forgotten you and the summer we played together, until I ran across a picture of you? Even then, I probably wouldn't have made a point of hunting you down if I hadn't realized, later, that you were exactly the person I needed, the only one who could help me with something I . . . have to do."

Again, she tensed. She tried to hide it by sounding nonchalant. "Really? And what is that?"

Jase looked at her, then down at the table where he had spilled the sugar what seemed like a long time ago. He pushed it into a small heap with the side of his thumb.

Now, he knew, was the time to trust her instincts—and his own. She undoubtedly loved her grandmother as much as he had loved his. Surely, she'd be willing to help. Especially if it meant saving her grandmother from a harm greater than betrayal. Better, he thought, for Evelyn Landry to feel simply betrayed, than betrayed *and* bereft of a large portion of capital.

But, and this was the cruncher, would Shell insist on running immediately to her father with what he had to tell her?

Suddenly, he wasn't certain this was the right approach. Maybe he'd be better off trying to get through to Evelyn Landry on his own. But how?

He knew the success rate for that kind of operation. Chances were, the lady would deny any possibility of his being right and tell him to mind his own business. And why should she believe him over the man she was probably in love with? Even with an introduction, he knew he'd be scrambling in loose gravel, getting her to believe him.

"Jase," Shell said impatiently when he continued to look down at the table and play with the sugar. "I want answers."

He let out a long breath. They both laughed as his stomach growled. "Feed me," he said, "then I'll tell you."

"What?" she said, though she was already on her feet. "You lead up to something like that and then want to back off?"

He shrugged. "With another cup of coffee and some food under my belt, it'll be easier for me to explain."

"All right." She turned to the stove with more enthusiasm than she liked. Shouldn't she demand the explanation immediately? He could talk while she prepared some food. Why did she feel such intense relief at having it put off? What was she, some kind of ostrich?

No, of course not, she comforted herself. She was simply hungry, too, and whether he'd been expected or not, remembered or not, Jase O'Keefe was a guest in her home and an old friend. The least she could do was give him breakfast.

She topped off their mugs before poking through the dark refrigerator and pulling out things she knew wouldn't keep long. Quickly, she made two sandwiches, cut them, and set them on plates. "Spaghetti sauce or ham?" she asked.

He stared at her. "Spaghetti sauce? You make sandwiches out of cold spaghetti sauce?"

She handed him the ham and sat down again. "Sure." She took a big bite, chewed, and swallowed. "I like spaghetti-sauce sandwiches." Indicating his sandwich, she said, "Eat, O'Keefe."

He finished off the sandwich so quickly, she knew he'd been famished. She made him another, which he demolished with slightly less speed and more relish, then sat back in her chair, eyeing him steadily.

"Okay," she said, "how about that explanation?"

Her manner added, *And it better be good.*

He drew a deep breath, shoved his plate aside, and leaned one elbow on the table. "You remember my grandmother?"

She chewed her lower lip, perplexed. What could any of this have to do with his grandmother? "I . . . think so." She cast her mind back to that summer she and Jase had played together. He'd been staying with his grandmother in her cottage. All that she recalled was an impression of a small, busy lady who never seemed to stop moving. "Is she . . . ?"

"She died two years ago."

"I'm sorry. I'm sure you miss her."

"Yes." Again, he hesitated, scratching his bristly chin with one thumbnail as he studied her. "I was going through a box in her house, and I found a picture of us from that summer. We were both hanging by our knees from the branch of a tree. Gran had dated and labeled it, 'Jase and his little friend Shirley (Shell) Landry, playing possum.'"

"But," she said, "since that was twenty-three years ago and several thousand miles away in another country, how in the world did you track me down here? And why?" She fixed him with a suspicious look. "'Track down' being the phrase you used last night."

"Yes." He swallowed hard and went on. "Once I saw your name and remembered you, you kept cropping up everywhere."

Shell's well-honed instincts for danger sprang up. "Excuse me, but I keep a very low profile. I do not 'crop up' everywhere, or anywhere except in my bookstore."

"And at your father's annual Christmas bash."

She stared, and he went on. "You were photographed with your grandmother arriving for that party."

She sat up straight and slammed her hand flat onto the table, jangling cups and spoons. "*Damn!* I hate newspapers!" she exploded. "Poking, prying, invading people's privacy, never letting up for—"

Seeing his concerned frown, she grabbed for control, struggling to even out her breathing and gulping back what could have turned into a tirade. But she silently continued to condemn the gossipy reporter who'd had that picture published, and Jase for having seen it. But wait a minute. How could he have seen it, unless he'd had a North America–wide clipping service on her case before it was published? A lot of trouble to go to to track down a "girlfriend" who'd been less than seven years old the last time he'd seen her.

"That was a year ago," she said. "And since when do photos from the 'around town' type columns in our local papers make it by wire service all the way to Los Angeles? My father's party simply wasn't that important in the scheme of world affairs. Try another one, O'Keefe. That one didn't quite fly."

"The clipping didn't make it to Los Angeles," he said. "I didn't see it until a week ago, and it took me from then until yesterday to discover your address."

She felt hollow and frightened. "How—how did you get that?"

He grinned evilly and brushed an imaginary mustache beneath his nose. "Ve haff our vays, ve schpies."

He wasn't going to tell her. She pulled air in through a tight chest. Faint and far away, she could hear Ned working with a chain saw, clearing the road, making it possible to get this man off Piney Point as soon as the Department of Highways filled in the washout. In the meantime she'd simply have to be extremely careful. She might have known Jase O'Keefe when they were children, but that didn't mean she had to trust him now. Or that she could.

Jase gazed at her. Her face was white, showing those freckles he'd remembered, and her green eyes were too large and looked hunted as she tried to hide a frantic expression that bordered on panic. Astounded, he realized she was afraid. Afraid of him? But why?

"All right," she said tautly. "The hunt's over. Now what do you want from me?"

Absurdly, he wanted to gather her close and promise her that she had nothing to fear from him, or from anyone else as long as he was near. Equally absurdly, he wanted to promise always to be near.

"I want to escort you to your father's Christmas party this year."

"What?" Her indignation didn't quite hide the relief he saw wash over her. A hint of color returned to her face, forming a pair of bright flags high on her cheekbones.

"If you know my dad," she said, her voice tense and angry, "you must also know that I never take a date to his party."

"I don't know your father. I've never met him."

"No?" She sat back and crossed her arms over her chest. "So what's your angle, O'Keefe? If you've never met my father, why do you want to go to his Christmas party?"

He met her gaze. "I want to meet your grandmother—or, more specifically, her new boyfriend."

She stared at him in confusion for several seconds before she let her arms relax onto the table. "Sterling Graves?" she asked. "You want to meet Sterling? But why? I mean, why at my dad's party? Sterling's from Palm Springs. You're from Los Angeles. Surely, you don't have to come all this way to get invited to the same party as Sterling Graves."

"I don't simply *want* to meet him. I *need* to meet him, and not as a man from Los Angeles. If I go to that party as your friend, introduced as someone you've known for years, he won't have cause to doubt me or my credentials or my reason for being there."

"And he would have otherwise?" Shell drew in a deep breath and fixed a hard stare on him. "What are you up to? Who are you, that he might not want to meet you 'as a man from Los Angeles'? If Sterling prefers not to meet you, why do you imagine for one minute that I'd slip you in under false pretenses? As I'm sure you know, since you know that my dad has an annual Christmas party, its guest list is exclusive, and outsiders are never, never included. And that goes for you, long-lost and sadly forgotten friend or not."

Important, influential guests attended her father, Elwin Landry's, party. They were able to relax in the knowledge that security was tight, that no one, neither fellow guest nor member of the catering staff, could enter the house or grounds that one night of the year without his or her background having been long known to Elwin, or rigorously examined by people he trusted. No one who wanted to work there again or attend as a guest would dare betray that trust.

And his daughter, who loved him, wouldn't even consider it.

"Yes," Jase said. "I do know all that. That's why I'm here with you now. And I'm not a stranger to you, remember. What I'm hoping is that through you, I'll be admitted, not be looked upon as an outsider, exactly as that bastard Graves will attend with your grandmother as one of the select group."

Shell stiffened her spine. "Sterling Graves might well become my stepgrandpa. That's why he's not being treated as an outsider. And why do you need to meet him?"

"Number one," Jase said evenly, "is to get his fingerprints so I can prove to myself that he really is the man I'm after. I'm ninety-nine percent convinced, but there is one small element of doubt. After your father's party, I'll know one way or the other, and be able to proceed with what I must do or back off and take my search elsewhere."

Shell gazed at him for a long moment, then got up, feeling unsteady and unsure on her feet. "Fingerprints?" She edged past him into the living room. As she added wood to the stove, she remembered Jase's terrible scars, the questions she'd had about them, and about him, in the night. Now was the time to ask, to demand an answer, not some glib evasion.

She spun and looked at him. "Search? For what? What are you, Jase? Some kind of a cop, or—"

"Or a crook?" He shook his head. "No. What I am, Shell, is a man out to nab the crook who bilked my grandmother of her life's savings and probably hastened her death. The man who I believe intends to do something similar to your grandmother."

For a long moment she said nothing, could say nothing. When her breath came back, she whispered, "You're kidding."

He shook his head.

"Why would you make that kind of accusation about a man you obviously don't even know? I mean, you have to get his fingerprints to be sure. What kind of qualifications do you have for comparing fingerprints?"

He struggled to his feet, hitching the blanket up and tighter around him, and walked over to her. Standing before her, he gnawed at his lower lip as he searched for the right words. "I have . . . connections who can make a good enough comparison to assure me," he said finally. "I can't prove it yet, but I truly believe the man is a con artist, Shell. I believe he's about to take your grandmother for a bundle, the way he did mine just before she died."

Shell couldn't breathe for a long, painful moment. She had to reject what he said. It was ludicrous to think it could be true. "You're out of your mind!"

"I am not." He pounded one fist into the other, nearly losing his blanket. "Dammit, Shell, I believe my grandmother died of a broken heart after Sterling Graves took her money and left her more or less at the altar."

Shell slipped past him to the table, turning her head to keep her eyes on him. "But, Jase, that's . . . well, that's impossible! Sterling Graves is a perfectly honest man, a true gentleman, old-fashioned, courtly. I spent a week with my grandmother in Palm Springs in the fall, and I met him. She owns a condo there in a seniors complex. He lives in the same facility, and apart from the fact that I liked him, that's not a place that lets in deadbeats. If a person's not invited, the guards at the gate don't admit him. Places like that also check the residents' credentials before they move in. He's the genuine article, and he's also the best thing that's happened to my grandmother in many, many years.

"And he can't be a con man," she added in triumph. "He comes from a good family back East, a family my grandmother has known since she was a girl. She knew *him* when she was a girl. They went to the same high school. She attended college with one of his sisters."

He lifted a hand. "Shell—"

She shook her head violently. "No. You're completely wrong about him, and I won't have my grandmother upset by you or anybody else making unfounded accusations about a man she's very, very fond of. Dad and I both hope the two of them will get married soon."

Jase braced himself on the back of his chair. "They won't be getting married, Shell. Sterling Graves, as he calls himself this year, never marries his marks. He simply charms the pants off them and takes their money and disappears."

"Ma-arks?" She made two angry syllables of the word. "You're crazy, you know, if you think my grandmother is a 'mark' for anybody! She's a bright, canny lady who's been around the block more than a time or two, and she's been protecting her money quite successfully since my grandfather passed away. Believe me, if she didn't trust Sterling Graves implicitly, she wouldn't have a thing to do with him, no matter how charming he might be."

With a haughty tilt to her chin, Shell grabbed their plates and cups off the table, swept the remains of her sandwich into the garbage, and all but dropped the dishes into the sink.

Spinning around with a wet cloth in her hand, she glared at Jase. "And one more thing. 'Lady' is the operative word in that description of my grandmother, O'Keefe. Evelyn Briggs Landry is a lady of the old school, and no man would charm 'the pants,' as you so crudely put it, or anything else off her, unless she was his lawfully wedded wife." She didn't quite add *so there*, but it was implicit in her tone.

Angrily, she scrubbed the tabletop, then paused in midswipe with the cloth, shooting him a frowning look. "What do you mean, 'calling himself this year'?"

Five

Jase took the cloth from her and tossed it over her shoulder to the sink. "Sit down, Shell. Please?"

She complied, still scowling, and he gratefully eased himself back onto his chair. "The man who calls himself Sterling Graves was not born with that name," he said quietly. "Maybe your grandmother knew a boy by that name when she was a girl, but he's long dead, and she obviously doesn't know it. I do, because the minute I learned what name he was using, I checked it out. I have the written proof in my Jeep."

"Convenient," Shell said, "since your Jeep is facedown in the middle of the creek, and all Ned was able to pull out was your bag and computer."

Jase's look of consternation broke on a smile. "Computer, right. I've got all the stuff on that too. Just wait one minute, and I'll show you." He opened the lid and switched on the computer. After a moment he sighed disgustedly and flipped the switch back and forth several times. "Dead!" He slammed the lid shut. "Dammit, Shell, you have to believe me. He's merely assumed that persona so he can earn her trust."

He seemed so sincere, Shell wanted to believe him. Only she knew Sterling, liked him. "Jase, honestly, your theory's crazy. Nobody would take such a stupid risk. If my grandmother really did attend the same school as Sterling Graves and go to college with his sister, then anybody other than the real Sterling would be off his noodle to pretend to be him. I mean, what if she'd kept in touch with the sister and been told of Sterling's death?"

"I believe the man does his homework well before he ever approaches his mark." When her mouth compressed and she sucked in an angry breath, he rushed on before she could object to the term again.

"If, by some chance, she had heard that Sterling was dead, he'd have laughed and quoted Mark Twain. Your grandmother, unlike me, probably wouldn't have bothered to check it out by calling the sister, or researching back copies of newspapers for obituaries, or requesting a death certificate from the state registry of births, deaths, and marriages. The innocent never do. But my bet is he knew before he went within ten miles of her that she hadn't kept in touch with Sterling Graves's family, that in fact she'd know nothing about the man, or even really remember him."

"Well, there you have it," Shell said definitively. "If she hadn't remembered him, she'd have been coolly polite and extricated herself from him at the earliest possible moment. My grandmother is a very wealthy widow. She's not stupid, Jase."

"*Would* she extricate herself politely? Can you be certain of that? As I said, the man is charming. He makes his living doing what he does. How do you know how your grandmother might respond to that kind of smooth operator? Have you ever seen her under those kinds of circumstances?"

"You mean, such as on a date?" Shell laughed with little humor. "Of course not. Well, not until recently. My grandmother didn't date after her husband died. She remained true to his memory for years."

She twisted her hands together. "That's why we were all so pleased when she struck up a friendship with Sterling. He claims to have loved her from afar when they were kids. He's a bit younger than she is, but Grandma says, at their age, what does that matter? They plan to go on a cruise together right after New Year's. In separate cabins," she added, "in case you're thinking otherwise."

"Shell, I'm sure your grandmother's morals are befitting a lady of her age and background. It's the morals of the man calling himself Sterling Graves that concern me. Can't you see? All these years she's been careful, rebuffed men who tried to get close, and suddenly she's fallen for someone and is planning on going away with him when she's known him—what?—two months?"

Shell worried the sleeve of her red sweater between her finger and thumb, staring down at it as if it had a stain she could rub away. "When you put it like that . . ." She looked up at him, clearly disturbed. "All right. Tell me more."

A trickle of relief ran through Jase. Maybe he was making some progress here. "I believe his name is—or was when he knew my grandmother— Martin Francis. Of course, it could be almost anything. Martin Francis is as unlikely to be the name he was born with as Sterling Graves."

"What makes you think the man who bilked your grandmother is Sterling Graves? How did you connect him and Martin Francis?"

"I've been tracking him for nearly a year and a half now, and I think he's rooked at least twelve other ladies in the past ten years. His M.O. is to buy a condo in a retirement community, pick a mark, then check her out in painstaking detail."

"How can he do that? As I said, my grandmother doesn't give out information indiscriminately. She's a very private person."

Jase nodded. He'd already learned that himself. "My suspect's a computer whiz. One of the few geriatric hackers in the world. He's broken into more data bases than you'd even suspect exist. He uses tax records, vital statistics, bank and credit-card data, everything he can access—legally or illegally—from the all-too-massive amount of information that's been compiled on each one of us, whether we try to keep our lives private or not.

"He ascertains that his victim is a widow. He already knows she's wealthy, or she wouldn't be living in such a place. He discovers her maiden name, where she was raised, what schools she attended, and who her friends were. And," he added after a significant pause, "who her friends were not."

Shell felt cold. Sterling Graves was, indeed, a "computer whiz." In only a few hours he had reprogrammed her entire stock-control system for her by modem, making it incredibly easy to use. But did that make him a "geriatric hacker"? Weren't hackers teenage nerds with fantastic IQs and no conscience?

"So you see," Jase went on, "if Sterling Graves and his sister were acquaintances of your grandmother's, but not friends, then he'd be fairly safe in assuming the Graves persona."

Shell blinked slowly as she assimilated what he'd said. Unwillingly, she had to admit he was making sense. "Yes," she said finally. "I see how it would be possible for him to wriggle into Grandma's confidence using a trick like that, and of course you're right. She probably wouldn't think to check him out. Why would she, since she already knew him, even if it was a long time ago?"

She chewed on her lip for a moment. "And you think he's been doing this for years? Why hasn't he been caught?"

"Mainly because he's careful whom he chooses as his mar—his prey. A con man's victims seldom complain. They're ashamed to let anyone, most of all their families, know how stupid they believe they've been and how much money they've lost. What they don't understand is that stupidity was not their problem. Love was, and trust, and quite likely a deep need to assuage their loneliness."

Shell swallowed hard, thinking of how often her grandmother begged her to come and spend more time with her, either in her Vancouver apartment or her Palm Springs condo. "You're my only granddaughter," she would say. "You have competent help in your bookstore. Take more time off. I wish you wouldn't spend so much time buried up there in the woods. After all, your mother has Maureen."

Had her insistence on "burying" herself contributed to her grandmother's loneliness? Had that helped set her up for a man like the one Jase described?

"He's also careful not to leave any pictures of himself behind," Jase said. "He dislikes having his photograph taken, managing to turn away at the crucial moment. Before he leaves, he lifts any pictures that might have been taken despite his precautions."

Shell remembered how Sterling had sneezed when she'd taken a photograph of him and her grandmother beside the pool. He'd whipped out a large white handkerchief that hid most of his face, then accidentally knocked her camera into the water before she could try to take another. He'd apologized, of course, and bought her a new, and much better, camera despite her protests that he didn't need to. But he had forgotten to buy film, too, and she'd returned home the next day without photographs of her week in Palm Springs.

"How did you find all this out?" she asked Jase.

"I'd been away while my grandmother was seeing him, so I never met him. But she told me what had happened. She was so ashamed, so heartbroken, and felt so betrayed, she had to talk to someone." He shrugged and watched his thumbnail track along the edge of the table. "And she knew I'd understand."

Shell felt a heaviness in her chest. Jase O'Keefe understood betrayal. And heartbreak? And shame? Why? When? Who? Mai-Lee?

Lifting his head he went on. "She'd always kept favorite photographs in a box in her bedroom closet, close by in case of fire, instead of in her albums down in the living room. Since Martin never knew about the box, he missed a full-face shot of himself."

"And that photo led you to Sterling?"

"Not directly and not immediately. She didn't show me the picture so that I could find the man, but to help me understand why she'd fallen so hard. He is a good-looking fellow. Thick silver hair, always impeccably groomed, a charming smile, and a body many men forty years younger would envy."

Worry rose within Shell. That described Sterling to a T. Except he had a thick, bushy mustache that twitched beguilingly when he smiled. His blue eyes always twinkled merrily, as if he were about to burst into a rollicking, possibly bawdy song.

"Gran refused to let me go to the local police even when I begged her to, to keep the man from harming other people. It wasn't until after she died, less than six months after Martin Francis left her, that I decided to get the guy myself."

"How?" She stared at him, her heart racing. "How can you expect to do it alone?"

He drew a deep breath, looking at her speculatively, as if wondering how far to go with his explanation. His mouth tightened to a hard line as he apparently made up his mind.

"I'm not doing it alone, Shell. I have the backing, unofficial but there nonetheless, of my superiors in the FBI. And the resources."

Her breath left her in a whoosh. "FBI . . . ?" All his scars now made sense, the physical, visible ones and those that gave him nightmares.

"My superiors said there wasn't enough evidence to go on, and even if there had been, they'd have assigned the case to someone else. So I tendered my resignation and took up the search myself." When she said nothing, he added, "They didn't accept my resignation. I'm on indefinite leave of absence."

Shell struggled to accept all that he'd said, to accept Jase and what he had become—a scarred, determined lawman, so different from the boy out of the past, a boy who had wanted adventure.

It seemed he had found it. And then some.

"Is there more evidence?" she asked. She wanted so badly for him to say yes. "Won't the FBI take over your investigation now?" Let someone else shatter her grandmother's heart, if that was what had to be done!

"No. I still don't have enough. After all, the only witness I knew to his crimes is . . . gone."

She reached across the table and touched his hand. He still grieved for his grandmother.

"I understand. So you're looking—have been looking—for another witness."

"Witnesses," he corrected her. "The minute Gran told me the whole story, I knew she couldn't have been his only victim. His method was too pat, too practiced, for him to have been an opportunist acting for the first time.

"She lived in Florida," he continued, "in a seniors development similar to the one your grandmother lives in. Since she'd told me exactly how he'd approached her, I went to other such places, showing that photo around, asking lots of question. Every so often I'd get lucky, and someone would remember his face, but the name was always different. No one would admit to having had personal dealings with him, but sometimes someone would suggest another place to search, another widow to question."

"But you've found no real witnesses in two years?"

He shook his head, sending a sweep of thick hair across his brow. Impatiently, he shoved it back. "I tracked him to the West Coast and set up my base in Los Angeles last year. After months of searching, I finally found him in Palm Springs last week. I learned from one of your grandmother's neighbors that a man called Sterling Graves, who looked very much like the man in my photo, had flown up here with her to attend her son's annual Christmas party. The neighbor boasted that she'd met Evelyn's son, that he was the man who'd almost single-handedly discovered what was happening with that commercial bank and the South American drug money and put a stop to it."

He grinned and tapped the back of her hand with one finger. "*That* made the Los Angeles papers.

"And that's why I came up here," he continued.

"I was following Sterling, and even after I knew your grandmother's name, I hadn't made the connection between you and the name Landry. Originally, I was going to go to your father, but while doing more research on him after I got here, I saw the picture of you and your name, Shell, in a back issue of the newspaper. I realized that your relationship to Evelyn Landry would provide exactly the introduction I needed. After all, it had to be you. The name Shell isn't common."

"No kidding." She leaped up, too agitated to sit still, and shoved her chair under the table. She stood there, gripping its back. It all seemed too pat. Too easy. What guarantee did she have that Jase O'Keefe was who he said he was? What if he was the one trying to run a scam of some sort? She had to admit it was an odd coincidence, a con man supposedly targeting both of their grandmothers. And he'd appeared so unexpectedly, a figure purportedly out of her past, exactly the method he claimed Sterling Graves had used on her grandmother.

Except . . . she did know him. She did remember him. Sort of. Long before he'd told her any of this, she'd found his face familiar, and she certainly did remember that incident with the live crabs and the candies.

"Why don't we go right to the police?" she asked, conscious of the note of pleading in her tone. "We have this little organization up here, Jase, that you might not have heard of. It's called the Royal Canadian Mounted Police. I believe they have a reputation of enjoying some small success in catching criminals. People have said of them,

'They always get their man.' Or if not them, let's bring my dad in on it."

He shook his head. "Sterling Graves has done nothing criminal to your grandmother as yet, so the RCMP won't be any more able to act than the FBI. What I want is to be on the scene before he does do anything, to warn her and seek her cooperation, so that when he makes his move, I can get the proof I need in order to bring in the right people."

He leaned forward, his eyes intense, his voice taut with barely controlled passion. "I want proof." He drew in an angry breath over clenched teeth. "No. Proof alone is not enough. I want to catch him in the act. I want to nail that man to the cross, Shell! And if I went to your father and managed to convince him, what are the chances that he'd leap in like a one-man S.W.A.T. team, as he did in South America, and scare Sterling away before he does anything actionable?"

"Pretty good," Shell admitted, still frowning in indecision.

Jase rose, too, and paced toward her. He put one hand on her shoulder and held her in front of him. "You are my only safe and sure link to the man, Shell. I need your cooperation. And your grandmother's. If she'll give it."

Shell bristled. "If you can convince her that Sterling is what you say he is, then of course she'll help you! She'll want to nail him to the cross as much as you do."

"I hope so, but I know how slim that chance is. Don't forget, there have been others, all of whom have angrily denied any association with the man.

It's that element of shame, Shell. They don't want the world to know they were taken in."

He drew in an unsteady breath and blew it out hard. "Don't you see? That's why I have to get a solid make on him before he gets to your grandmother. Help me, Shell! Help me stop this man so I can get on with my life!"

Shell steeled herself against giving into his impassioned plea before she'd had time to think it through. Shrugging out from under his hand, she spun toward the sink, where she put the plug in the drain and squirted in some soap.

"Shell?" He followed her. "I have to know. Will you help me?"

"I don't know!" she exploded, whirling back to face him. "What if you're wrong? What if I have to break my grandmother's heart for nothing more than a suspicion on your part?"

"I promise you. Your grandmother will know nothing of this until I'm positive he's the one I want."

Shell gnawed on her lower lip as she searched his face. She could see that he was convinced already. Either that or he was a talented actor. "All right," she said finally. "I have to admit that what you've told me could be true. If it is, of course I want to help. But I'll need to think about it for a while."

She slipped past him to the living room. A kettle of hot water sat on the stove, and she carried it back to the kitchen.

He watched, frowning, as she poured the water into the sink, making a froth of suds bubble up from under the plates.

"Shell, don't spend too much time thinking, okay? There's no telling when the man might strike. He may have done so already. Even today, your grandmother could be cashing in debentures at his request. The scam he pulled on my grandmother was pretending to be an officer of the bank and needing cash 'to catch a man defrauding innocent women.'"

Shell set the kettle on the useless electric range. "There is nothing either of us can do until the road is repaired, or until the phones are hooked up again. In the meantime we'll simply have to be patient and trust my grandmother, who is, as I said, a canny, cautious lady. She won't do anything before year's end. She'd hate to miss out on a cent of interest."

Dismissing the subject, she tapped the kettle with a fingernail. "There's plenty of hot water left in here, and a package of fresh razors in the bathroom. Feel free to use them to shave."

Sighing impatiently, Jase snatched the kettle, hitched up his blanket, and limped toward the bathroom. He slammed the door. Hard.

Shell washed the dishes, her shoulders slumped, her mind whirling. Could what Jase had told her possibly be true? And even if it was, what reason was there to think her grandmother would be taken in?

She was deep in thought when a cheerful voice called, "Good morning, Shirl! Are you busy?"

Shell spun to see her mother in her electric wheelchair rolling into the kitchen off the ramp that accessed the back door. Lil wore a bright yellow jacket with a vibrant print silk scarf at her throat, gray slacks, and black leather gloves. Her short silver-shot dark hair had been whipped by the same cold wind that had put a glow into her cheeks and a sparkle in her brown eyes.

"Lil!" Shell's voice cracked as she cast an apprehensive look at the bathroom door. "You shouldn't be here! You have to leave. Now!" Grasping the handles of her mother's chair, she turned it around and pushed it back the way it had come, her heart hammering in her chest, her head spinning with fear.

Lil was having none of that. She clamped on the brakes. Rubber tires gripped the tiles, bringing the chair to an abrupt halt. "I'm here," she said with a laugh, twisting around to look up at her daughter. "And you can't get rid of me now.

"Anyway," she added, her gaze following Shell's, which was fixed on the turning porcelain knob of the bathroom door, "what are you trying to hide, darling? Have you got some gorgeous hunk stashed away in there?"

On cue, Jase stepped out, freshly shaven, his hair damp, his torso bare, looking great even under all the bruises. His green blanket trailed around his bare feet.

Shell groaned softly and covered her eyes with one hand.

Lil gaped, then smiled that delightful, teasing smile that had first captivated the world four decades earlier. "Why, Shirl." She put her chair into gear and rolled forward slowly, never taking her eyes off Jase. "For the second time in your life, you've managed to surprise me. Not to mention delight me.

"The first time," she went on, clearly addressing Jase, "was when she was born. I was certain she had to be a boy. All the Landry family ever produced was boys. Her father was one of five brothers, and now she has three young Landry half-brothers, to say nothing of what seems like several dozen male cousins on her father's side. Of course, along with my immense surprise at having a girl was intense joy. I'd wanted a golden-haired daughter just like Shirley Temple for as long as I could remember. I named her Shirley Elizabeth, for two of the women I most admired in all the world. She's exactly what I had yearned for. I used to dress her in the prettiest things and—" Shell pressed her fingers against her mother's shoulder, and Lil drew a deep breath, letting it out slowly.

"But I'm talking too much, aren't I? I always do when I meet someone new. It's because I see so few fresh faces. Shirl, introduce me to your friend."

Shell gulped. "This is Jason O'Keefe," she managed to say, her voice a croak of dismay. "Jase, this is my mother, Lil Harris." Silently, she prayed he wasn't an old-movie buff. Years of living with multiple sclerosis had changed Lil greatly. Still, enough of her beauty shone through the lines of pain brought on by the debilitating disease, and her—and Shell's—greatest fear was that she might be recognizable to someone who would tell the world where she was.

And why.

Shell risked a glance at Jase. Hanging on to his blanket with his left hand, he stepped forward to shake the hand Lil had extended to him. "I'm pleased to meet you, Mrs. Harris."

"It's 'Miss,'" she said. "I've never been married. But call me Lil. I much prefer it."

He smiled and released her hand. "I believe we have met, Lil, when I was a small boy, one summer in Rhode Island."

Lil shot an inquiring glance at Shell, who could say nothing sensible at the moment. All she wanted to do was scream, or run, or hide her head, preferably in her mother's lap. Her heart beat too high, too fast, in her throat. Her palms were clammy. Her stomach was churning. She felt exactly as she had when she was six and some stranger had poked a camera into her face, exploding the world into bright shards of light.

"We've met?" Lil said, readily taking up the slack. "Really? Rhode Island . . . that was a long time ago. I'm surprised you remember me."

Jase looked momentarily uncomfortable. "I'm afraid I don't remember you. What I remember is playing with Shell, and I recall in the vaguest way that she lived with her mother. I don't think I saw much of you."

Lil smiled again, gaily. Shell could feel her relief. She only wished she could share it. "Probably not," Lil said. "I wasn't very sociable that summer, if I remember." She patted her wheelchair arm. "I was developing MS at the time, although I didn't know it, and felt extremely ill. The disease has had a slow progression, though, for which I'm grateful. I'm in a nice, solid remission now and feeling much more congenial, so why don't you let me make it up to you for my past neglect? I was just about to tell Shirl that I'm getting together a blackout party for luncheon. Why don't you get dressed and join us?"

"Lil, no!" Shell managed to find her voice. "You—we—you can't do that. You're not—"

"Nonsense, darling." Lil patted Shell's hand, gazing up at her with the big, deep brown eyes that had made more than one man fall in love with her image on the movie screen. "I'm having a very good day for once, and I mean to enjoy it. Maureen is making a huge pot of soup, so as I said, I came to invite you for lunch. Ned said you wouldn't be able to get to work today. I'm going to ask him, too, especially since he had to leave Nola back in town with her sister, and with your friend here, we can make a real party of it."

Lil loved parties. At one time in her life, the smallest event had been excuse enough. Now, though, the events were scarce, and her strength too unpredictable for many "occasions."

"No," Shell said. She hated to refuse, but she had to. Jase was, after all, from Los Angeles, where Hollywood legends held far more importance than they did in any other part of the world. If he wasn't aware now of who her mother was, he very likely would be when all the sensationalism and speculation about her disappearance was rehashed in a few weeks, along with photographs. Even if he didn't recognize Lil Harris as the long-missing Lilianne, he'd surely connect Shell with Shirley Elizabeth, Lilianne's little daughter, who had gone missing at the same time.

It was one thing having impromptu parties with friends they all knew and trusted, but it was another thing inviting a perfect stranger into Lil's home where her two Oscars stood proudly on the mantelpiece.

What was the matter with Lil that day? Shell wondered. Why was she sitting there beaming at Jase, who was beaming back like a bloody jack-o'-lantern, clearly responding to that once-world-famous smile? Maybe recognizing it! Didn't Lil realize the danger she was in?

"Lil, please," Shell begged in a strained voice. "Jase, let me speak to my mother in private, will you?"

"Yes. Of course, Shell. I'll just go—"

Lil reached out and caught a handful of his blanket, holding him fast. "Shirl, darling, don't be like that. Jase is your friend, isn't he?"

She twitched the blanket and sent a twinkling smile flitting between the two of them. "It appears to me that he's a *very good* friend, so of course we must include him in our little luncheon party. Right, Jase?"

Jase gently tugged the blanket from her fingers and scooped up the bag Ned had brought in. "Right, Lil," he said. "And thank you. I'd be delighted."

Shell glared at him. "How far do you think you'll get without shoes, O'Keefe? You ended up here barefoot."

He flapped a hand at her. "I never let minor details like that worry me when a beautiful woman has asked me to lunch. We'll be there, Lil. With bells on." He paused for effect. No way was he going to tell Shell that he had another pair in his bag. "If not shoes."

Lil's rich, full-throated laugh was his reward.

Six

"Why didn't you want me to go to your mother's house?" Jase asked as they walked home that night. They followed a path between the two houses, lit by the flashlight Shell carried.

Dammit, she thought, he saw altogether too much. She considered denying his allegation but shrugged. Why resort to a phony denial that he wouldn't believe anyway? She hadn't wanted to take him there. That it had turned out as well as it had was no thanks to her abilities to protect her mother. To her eternal relief, Maureen, her mother's dear friend and longtime companion, had seen them coming up the ramp and had the presence of mind to whisk the gold statuettes away. Jase had not seen them, had asked no questions that couldn't be answered easily, and had spent most of the ensuing hours entertaining them, rather than the other way around.

"Lil isn't well," she said. "Surely, you could see

that." Then, almost grudgingly, she added, "Though I must say she enjoyed your company and your stories. All that laughter seemed to add to rather than deplete her strength. She hasn't managed to stay up so late in ages."

"There now. See how trustworthy I am?" Jase asked, laughing. "My mission in life is to keep ladies from wanting to go to bed. What better recommendation could you ask? Or," he added, "could Ned ask? I felt like Jack the Ripper when he came in to find me there with you. Are all your neighbors so protective of you?"

Shell bit her lip, thinking of the outraged expression on Ned's face when he had arrived for lunch and seen Jase ensconced in an overstuffed armchair, his injured leg on a footstool and an attentive audience of three women avidly listening to a hilarious story of one of his college escapades.

None had been more fascinated, more enchanted, than Lil, Shell thought, frowning. Somehow, they were going to have to find ways to protect Lil from herself as long as Jase was stranded on Piney Point. Even after Shell had managed to let her mother know that she and Jase were not lovers, that he had blown in with the storm and would be gone again almost as quickly, Lil continued to treat him as if he were Shell's beloved. No, more than that. As if he were Shell's intended.

And that was scary!

"Ned and Nola are 'all our neighbors,'" she said in response to his question. "Piney Point contains just our three houses, all of which belong to my mother and Maureen, and yes, he's very protective."

"I got the impression he hated to leave me alone with the three of you after lunch. And he certainly wasn't delighted to find me still there at dinnertime. He's more than protective. He's out to protect you from me personally."

"That's silly," she said. "Of course he's not."

That was only half-true. Ned was protective; he just wasn't protecting Shell. And he seemed to think it was through some negligence on her part that Jase was there. As if she'd had any choice in the matter!

She rolled her eyes; remembering her mother's comments, too, when she'd gone to Lil's bedroom to say good night.

"What a honey your Jase is," she'd whispered to Shell as they hugged. "I can't remember when I've met a nicer man, one who suited you more, and I can see that you like him a lot."

Before Shell could protest, Lil had added, "He likes you, too, baby doll, so see that you don't chase him away by being unnecessarily cautious." She'd pulled a scornful face. "That Ned. Really, the man takes things, and himself, far too seriously. See to it that you don't start acting like him, all right?"

Shell hadn't argued. Her mother was so tired, she'd told herself, she didn't know what she was saying. Unnecessarily cautious? Taking things too seriously? There was no such thing when it came to protecting Lil's privacy. That caution had been bred into her and had become so ingrained, she couldn't exist outside of its strictures. She wondered if her mother's disease had resumed its inexorable progress and was affecting her thought processes. It was completely unlike Lil to be as careless with a stranger as she had been with Jase.

No wonder Ned had been having fits.

From the time she was ten years old, Shell had been taught never to tell anybody much about herself, her parents, or her upbringing, particularly about how she had lived before coming to the Sunshine Coast and Piney Point. Yet all day Lil had been less than discreet in her choice of subjects for discussion. Ned and Shell and Maureen had shared more than one alarmed glance at some of her disclosures.

"Ned's . . . very old-fashioned," she said now in response to Jase's comment. "I don't suppose his finding you in my house this morning dressed only in a blanket did much to endear you to him. Don't take his actions personally. He'd have been that way no matter who you were."

Jase laughed. "Not true, Shell. He simply doesn't like me. Or trust me. And it all seems centered on my coming from California. It was my license plates far more than my state of undress that got his back up. Why, Shell? Is it because you and your mother lived there for a time? Did something happen there that makes Ned distrust Californians on her behalf and yours?"

Shell stumbled. That was too near the mark for comfort!

Jase steadied her, then caught her hand, holding on to it.

"No," she said quickly. "What could have happened? It's just that Ned has a—a strange attitude about tourists. To him, everyone who crosses the forty-ninth parallel is automatically suspect. Californians, of course, being the worst of the bad." She lowered her tone, sounding deeply condemning. "Useless parasites every one, brains either fried by too much sun or numbed by smog. Drug dealers, addicts, or AIDS carriers, if not all three."

She and Jase shared a laugh. She thought about twisting her hand free, but it felt nice—no, more than nice—to walk shoulder to shoulder with him, their fingers linked together. "I don't know how he deals with me," she continued. "I was born there, after all, lived there for the first ten years of my life."

"Ah, but your dual citizenship must have made all the difference."

"I suppose." She glanced up at him. "Don't let Ned get to you, Jase, please. He's like that with all strangers."

"He doesn't bother me in the least. And he's not alone in his attitude. I've found it all over the U.S. Californians are weird."

"But you aren't really one, are you? Didn't you say you'd lived in every state except Nebraska and Ohio?" It had been a throwaway comment over lunch, and when she'd tried to go back to it earlier, Jase had steered the conversation down another alley.

"That's right," he said, his tone nonchalant. "But I'm all Californian now, so there must be something wrong with me. I mean, who in his right mind would live on a geological fault and shrug off the idea that the entire state could end up in the Pacific Ocean in the blink of an eye?"

"Makes a person wonder, doesn't it?" Slipping her hand out of his, she asked, "Why are you so reluctant to talk about your childhood, Jase? I mean, especially to me. After all, I shared a couple of months of it." And why, she wondered, was she pressing him to do what she couldn't do in return?

Because, she had to acknowledge, she wanted to know him better, wanted to understand what made Jase O'Keefe tick.

It was more important than she liked.

He shrugged and came to a halt on the side of the path where rough-cut logs formed five steps down to the beach.

"It wasn't such a great childhood," he answered at last. "What's to talk about?"

He said nothing more, and they stood silent, listening to the slow, lazy swells curl and wash up over the gravel, then recede, rolling pebbles out with them in a gentle, rattling sound. Overhead, a three-quarter moon on the wane shone down between straggling, wind-streaked clouds. Shell turned off the flashlight, and as her eyes adjusted, she could see the waves on the beach, black with shining edges, gleaming under the moon. The navigation light on White Islet, half a mile offshore, blinked monotonously, warning ships away.

To get a little, she thought, you have to give a little.

"As you might have gathered from the conversation today," she said, "my childhood wasn't exactly modeled on a TV-sitcom family, either. At least your parents were married to each other. I didn't even know I had a father, let alone who he was, until I was ten and we moved up here."

He took her hand again and, still holding it, slipped it into his jacket pocket. "Mine weren't married very long. They divorced when I was five, Jenny four, and Marcus about two. After that, they traded us back and forth as if none of us mattered much more than the family camping gear, which also traveled from household to household when it was needed."

She squeezed his fingers. "Jase . . . I'm sorry."

"It's all right. I came to terms with it long ago. My dad called it 'getting along,' my mother, 'dealing with reality.'" He laughed, to show he really didn't care, though Shell knew he did. "Joint custody," he added. "What a crock. The courts that order it never ask the kids if they want to be human Ping-Pong balls. The only normalcy in my life was the times I spent with my grandmother."

"Such as that summer we played together. Your brother and sister weren't there. Why?"

"Because Jenny was with Dad, and Marcus was with Mom. I rebelled, so they sent me to Gran to get 'straightened out.'"

"Did it work?"

He chuckled. "Not appreciably. How about you? How did you and your mother come to be in Rhode Island that summer? Lil said she worked in the Los Angeles area."

"Why, uh, I guess we were . . . on vacation," she said lamely. She couldn't very well say "in hiding," which was closer to the truth.

Even now, thinking about it, she felt sick to her stomach, hearing again the shrill demanding voices, "Lilianne, was it alcohol or drugs?" "Were you drinking because Max Elkford left you for Marcy LeFave?" And the pictures of her mother on her hands and knees, hair awry, beautiful face streaked with tears, agony painted on every feature as she struggled to rise, flashed across Shell's memory.

She shuddered and forced the images away. "Can't people from the West Coast want a change of scene now and then?"

"I suppose." He paused, as if waiting for her to go on.

"Let's go in," she said. "I'm sure your pampered California bones must be frozen about now, to say nothing of your leg."

"They're not," he said, but followed her along the path.

Skeena bounded up to them as they neared the cottage. Shell turned the flashlight on the dog and bent to brush a litter of twigs off her black fur. When she'd had enough grooming, Skeena turned and loped up the ramp to the house, nearly knocking Shell to the ground. She would have fallen, had not Jase's arm swept around her and held her pinned to his chest.

"Steady." His voice was gruff.

"I'm all right." Hers was breathless.

He touched her hair, brushing it back from her face. "Are you?" She felt a tremor in his fingers, felt his heart hammering hard and fast under her palm as she pressed it to his chest, half to hold herself apart from him, half because she couldn't pull it away.

"Yes . . ." she said, but it came out as a soft, aching whisper as she gazed into the fathomless darkness of his eyes.

"That's funny," Jase said. "I'm not." He drew her closer, stroking her hair with one rough hand as he pressed her head to his chest. No, he wasn't all right. What he was doing was insane. The way he reacted to this woman was wrong and had to stop. He should set her away from him, force himself to go inside the house and out of this tempting darkness, to where walls and light and commonplace surroundings would put his mind back on track and make his body behave. So, why wasn't he doing any of that?

Because *she* wasn't moving! She was standing there, not quite leaning on him, but he was totally aware of her shape, her heat, the outline of her breasts through the thickness of her sweater and jacket. His jacket was open, and her hand rested on his chest, separated from his skin by nothing more than his shirt. Was she still there because she, like him, simply couldn't move?

"Shell . . . ?" His voice sounded rough, rasping.

"What?" Hers sounded bemused, and he groaned, grabbing a fistful of her hair and tilting up her face.

Shell sucked in a deep breath, seeking the strength to push herself away from him. As if he sensed her intention, he tightened his hand in her hair, then released it. To her horror, Shell found herself melting against him, soaking up the warmth of his body, breathing deeply of his scent.

"You do something to me, you know," he said.

Her blood thrummed loudly in her ears, almost blocking the sound of his ragged breathing. His arm slid farther around her, and his hand caressed her shoulder, moving over her collar until his fist rested just under her chin. Its faint pressure urged her to obey the dictates of her own desires, to reach up and take the kiss she knew he'd give her if she showed him she wanted it.

She leaned her head back. His hand was warm on her throat, his thumb hard under her chin. "Ah, Shell . . ."

"Shell!"

She stiffened at Ned's barking tone, then jerked away from Jase. To her dismay, her voice shook when she spoke. "H-hi, Ned. I . . . um, I thought you'd have been home in bed long ago." She cringed. Lord! She sounded guilty!

"It's late," Ned said. "I should be in bed. So should you." His flashlight bobbed as he came down the ramp from her door to join them on the path. "I've brought in enough wood to last the night. The stove's packed, and the fire's banked down. Should burn all right for a while."

"Th-thank you." Shell mentally cursed herself for sounding timid and embarrassed. She had been doing nothing wrong. Squaring her shoulders, she tipped her chin an inch higher. Dammit, she refused to act like a thirteen-year-old caught in a forbidden clinch by an oppressive father. Ned had no right to make her feel that way.

"I figured you'd be pretty cold," Ned said, "what with standing outside so long . . . talking." His tone suggested that he suspected talk had played little part in their activities.

He slid a disapproving glance at Jase. "Ain't California here, you know. People shouldn't hang around outside in the cold and damp at night."

He switched his gaze to Shell's face, half-illuminated by the twin beams of their flashlights reflecting off the white shell path. "You off to bed now, or do you want me to come in and light some lamps for you?"

"No, thanks, Ned." She managed a cool smile. Her mother was right. Ned took himself too seriously, although she knew he meant well. "I'm sure Jase and I can light a couple of lamps between us. You've spent enough time looking after me. You go on home now. I know you must be tired."

"The crick's gone down another foot or two," he said, addressing Jase. "I'll have your Jeep out by noon tomorrow. It looks like a write-off to me, but you can hike out to town and get a tow truck."

"Jase has an injured leg," Shell said. "He won't be hiking anywhere. Your car is on the other side of the washout. Can't you at least be civil enough to offer him a ride?"

Ned sniffed. "That leg didn't stop him hiking over to Lil's house." Before Shell could retort that the distances were much different, he turned away. His boots pounded heavily as he stomped along the path without so much as a "good night."

"See?" Jase said, staring after the older man. "I told you he had a personal dislike for me."

Shell sighed, shaking her head regretfully, then led the way up the wheelchair ramp to the back porch. As she reached for the doorknob, Jase caught her hand.

"No," he said. "Wait. Shell, I know this is none of my business, but I need to know. Does Ned have any . . . uh, right to his attitude?"

She stared at him. "What does that mean?"

He let her hand go and grasped her shoulders, turning her to face him. "I think you know what it means."

"I . . . Jase." She drew in a deep, tremulous breath. "No. No, of course not."

"There's no 'of course' about it. He's a man. You're a very lovely woman."

Her laugh came out sounding strained and metallic. "He's more than twenty years older than I." Dammit, she thought, she didn't like the direction this conversation was taking. Why were they having it? Why was she standing there listening to him?

He smiled. "An age difference has never been a problem before to my knowledge."

"He's also married!" she all but wailed.

Jase touched her cheek, unable to prevent himself, drawing a callused finger down her face from her eyebrow to her chin. "That doesn't always matter, either, Shell."

He felt the shiver that ran through her. "It would matter to me," she said quietly.

For a long moment he studied her in the faint moonlight. "Yes," he said finally. "Integrity is part of your soul, isn't it?"

"I hope so," she said, her voice scarcely above a whisper, then she ducked away from him and slipped inside.

Jase followed, inhaling deeply, appreciating the scents that greeted him. Entering Shell's house was like walking into a wall of aromatic heat. The scent of the Christmas tree hung pungently in the air, along with a tinge of alder smoke and some undefinable perfume that he suspected would always be where Shell was.

A strange sensation of homecoming struck him with throat-tightening intensity, though he had never before come home to the warmth of a fire and couldn't recall ever having a real tree for Christmas. Still, something primitive in him reveled in the welcome he felt in Shell's snug little cottage.

In silence they took off their jackets and shoes, then followed the beam of Shell's flashlight into the living room, where the two oil lamps waited. She handed him the flash so she could light a match, and he watched as the flame flickered, caught, and held, sparking a silver glitter of tinsel and reflecting in red, silver, green, and gold tree ornaments. And in Shell's eyes.

Fascinated, he stared at her, at her slender hands as she lit the other lamp. He felt the warmth of her body close to his, and controlled himself with difficulty. Damn, but he felt cheated out of a kiss that he needed. Each time he held her, he found it harder to let her go. In only twenty-four hours Shell Landry had got under his skin.

"Your hair looks pretty in lamplight." He heard the words before the thought had fully formed. She turned to him, startled.

Their gazes collided and locked. The dead match

fell to the table, rolled across it, and hit the floor with a noise far out of proportion to its size.

"Thank you." She looked away and fiddled unnecessarily with the height of the wick. The glow increased, and Jase watched the shadows leap and waver, as did too many emotions within him.

"Does anyone else have the right to object to my being here?" he asked.

She glanced warily at him. "You mean, like a man?"

He had to smile. "No, Shell. Not 'like' a man. A man, dammit." He wished he'd been able to temper the intensity in his voice, but it reflected the growing, grinding need in him.

Her breasts rose high under her red sweater as she drew in a deep breath. "No . . ."

"That's good."

"Jase . . ." Shell felt a protest rising up inside her, but it was negated by a surge of pure, hot desire as his hand moved over her hair, stroking down its length and pulling away the scarf with which she'd tied it.

"It was curly before," he said, sliding his hand over it again. "When you were a little girl."

She nodded jerkily, unable to tear her gaze away from his face. "As—as Lil said, she grew up admiring Shirley Temple. If I was ever a disappointment to her, it was because of my completely straight hair. She started having it permed even before I can remember. I didn't stop until I was in high school and wanted to grow it long and . . ."

Oh, Lord, she was talking too fast, too much. Why didn't she move away from him? Distance would surely alleviate this fast-growing, coiled-spring tension inside her. Her breath caught in her constricted chest. Her wobbly knees threatened to collapse, and her heavy eyelids wanted to drop down as he trailed his hand over her hair again. Through it. Fingers against her scalp, her neck, her shoulder . . .

The desire to run, to hide, dwindled. As she gazed at him, it seemed the two of them were cocooned in a small, sensual world with boundaries of darkness around which a thousand tempting dangers lurked.

"Shell," he murmured. He stroked her cheek with his thumb, confirming her belief that it was perilous to stand so close to him. She shuddered but still couldn't look away.

Dear Lord, Jase thought. He must have been out of his mind, thinking that coming indoors would make it easier not to give in to the temptations this woman presented. It was worse, far worse, inside, with the soft warmth of the wood stove wrapping around them, the gentle glow of the oil lamps casting mysterious shadows across her face and playing like liquid gold over her hair . . . her beautiful sleek, silky hair.

"I like it better this way," he said, lifting her hair and letting it fall as he turned her face toward his. "It's thick and rich-looking, and hangs like a heavy satin curtain around your shoulders when you leave it loose."

Shell could say nothing. She was trembling deep inside and knew that from this moment on the scent of wood fires, of Christmas trees, even the aroma of oil lamps, would evoke Jason O'Keefe for her. She sighed in response to the touch of his fingers in her hair, on the back of her neck. It reminded her of their kiss that morning, the stolen one in the night, and made her want it all over again. The feel of his lips, the hardness of his body, the strength of his arms. . . . His scent. His taste.

Him.

He outlined her left ear with one finger. "Shell," he said. "The name fits."

She gripped the corner of the table in both hands and stared down at the box of matches, the silver-and-black tube of the flashlight, the sprigs of leaves Nola had embroidered on the tablecloth. She tried to find a sense of normalcy in those things, tried to keep her mind under control when it insisted on winging off into a fantasy world peopled only by two humans who ached to be one.

One callused, masculine finger stroked down the side of her face, as it had outside. But here, in the intimacy of the house, the effect was even more galvanizing. "Your skin is the same delicate shade as the inside of a shell." He slowly slid that finger under her chin, lifting it, turning her face back toward him. "And as smooth."

She breathed in the scent of him, heard the soft sound of his breathing, and felt the warmth of his body close to hers. His other hand slid around her waist, and he turned her to face him fully.

"Last night," he murmured, "one of the first things I noticed was your hair, how glossy it is, how smooth. I wanted to touch it then and see if it felt as silky as it looks."

She tried to speak. Her lips parted, but no sound issued. He lifted several strands of hair and let them trickle out of his fingers, watching as they caught the light. She saw the shimmering movement reflected in his dark eyes. She saw herself there, saw her own uncertainty . . . and her own need, and knew he must see it too. Now, when she wanted to close her eyes to hide from him, they refused to obey her command. She stood there, caught in the web of his gaze.

His hand encircled her nape, drawing her closer until the tips of her breasts rested on his chest, softness against hardness, and their breaths mingled.

"Shell?" His voice was a dusky whisper, filled with intent.

"Jase . . ." Hers was a soft plea, but whether a plea for him to let her go or to continue, she couldn't tell. His other hand rested lightly on the small of her back, exerting no pressure. A deeper shudder ran through her. As if in answer, his fingers curled, pressing against her spine. He smiled down at her, then his thumb traced over her cheek. She trembled, feeling her will grow weaker and weaker, and stepped forward into the fullness of his embrace.

Jase closed his eyes as he lowered his head to hers, his heart hammering hard, loud, in his chest. His entire body vibrated as her breasts brushed his chest. Viscerally, he felt the tremulous breath she drew, and he pulsated from head to toe as she curved her hand around his jaw. The rasp of his whiskers was loud against her hand. The sound sent a shaft of regret through him, for his beard might mar her skin, but even that couldn't stop what was about to happen.

He was going to kiss her, taste her, feel her instant responses to him again. He had to kiss her. Nothing was going to stop him from doing what he needed to do, had needed to do all day.

Slowly, prolonging the pleasure, he slid his arms around her, drawing her into him. He reveled in the softness of her body, the scent of her, the sound of her quickly indrawn breath. Her instinctive quiver fed his desire, and he moaned softly. His palms flattened against the small of her back, fingers curving down and around over her firm buttocks. As his mouth brushed hers, he felt her lips part, and he took what she offered.

It was sweet and deep and so powerful, he groaned aloud, pulling her in tight to his hardness, moving against her. She softened, whimpered, slid her hands through his hair, and held him close. Lifting his head, he gazed down at her. Her eyes fluttered open. He smiled, then kissed them shut again before accepting the silent plea of her damp, parted lips.

Seven

Their breathing was hot and hard when they broke their kiss. They stared at each other, as if searching for the truth of what had swept—continued to sweep—through them in waves of awesome intensity.

"Jase . . ." Shell said, her voice choked, muted. She shook her head.

"I know. I know." He rested his forehead against hers, then as if he couldn't stop himself, snatched her into a hug so tight, she thought she might break in half. She didn't. She molded herself to him and pulled his head down, this time taking, not giving. He held nothing back from her. He was willing to let her have all she wanted of him, which was more, more, and yet more. . . .

Oh, Lord! Jase tore his mouth free and trailed it over her face, loving the satin of her skin, the scent of her hair, the small cries she made to tell him of her pleasure. She arched toward his hand as he found a full, firm breast. He cradled it, enjoying its warmth, its weight, even through the barrier of her clothing.

She shifted, wordlessly telling him what she wanted, what she needed. It was what he needed too. He stroked his hand down her side to her waist and slipped it under her sweater, feeling her abdomen ripple in response. Her skin was so soft, and he eagerly unhooked her bra and pushed it aside. She moaned, her body surging into his at the touch of his hand on her bare breast.

He caught her sound of delight in his kiss, and rolled an exquisitely taut nipple under his palm and between his fingers, then flicked it with his thumb until she shuddered. Her hips thrust forward, pressing against his in a rhythm that took his breath away. He gasped as desire burned through him, growing, aching, demanding release. He needed her. Had to have her. Couldn't live unless he had her under him, naked, open, taking . . .

He lifted his head and caught a handful of her hair, tilting her face up to his. He saw the dazed glow in her eyes, the need that so closely approached his. "I want you," he whispered, tugging her sweater up. He pulled it off over her head, then slid her bra down her arms. He wanted to see her naked in the lamplight and needed to take her breasts in his mouth. Needed her.

He skimmed both hands over her, molding her, holding her, gazing in delight at the flush that rose up over her chest, at the proud, jutting nipples, the rapid rise and fall of her breasts. He wet one nipple with his tongue, watched it gleam in the lamplight, then sucked it deep into his mouth as he lifted her against him.

"I want you," he repeated, his voice ragged as he struggled to tug his shirt from his waistband with one hand. "Now, Shell. Against me. Touching me. Now." He set her down, tore his shirt open, reached for her again, and grasped . . . air.

"No!" The word was a soft, explosive sound, like a sob. She had jerked away from him so suddenly and swiftly, he couldn't stop her. Folding one arm protectively over her breasts, she stared at him. She shoved her tangled hair away from her face and staggered back from him, leaving him alone and cold.

Shell's head was spinning, and her knees threatened to buckle. The deep pulsing inside her had made it almost impossible to wrench herself away, but she'd had no choice. She knew that. Something had shrieked at her, *Stop now! Get out of this before it's too late! To go on is crazy!*

She stared at Jase from five feet away. His chest heaved, as did hers. His hands clenched and unclenched at his sides. Black hair glistened damply where his shirt hung open, arrowing down his flat belly to his belt. She tore her gaze away from the bulge in the front of his jeans, sweeping it over his face. His eyes looked half-crazed, and his mouth hung partly open on a word he couldn't articulate. He snapped it shut and tried again.

"What?" he finally managed, but she took another step back as if he had threatened her. "What's . . . what went . . . wrong?"

She struggled to control her panting. She was hyperventilating, growing dizzy. "I . . . can't."

Can't what? she asked herself. Can't explain? Can't go further with this? Even she didn't know what she meant at the moment. She knew only that it had been too much, too big, too frightening, whatever it was that had sprung up between them. And he was a stranger. A stranger from California. Forbidden.

"Dammit, Shell—" Jase bit off the rest of what he'd been going to say and sank down onto the sofa. Leaning his elbows on his knees, he buried his face in his hands. He had never forced a woman in his life. And he had never felt more like doing so than he did at that moment. He breathed deeply, keeping a tight rein on his riotous emotions and the instincts that insisted he had only to touch her again, to hold her and kiss her and run his hands over her body, and she'd be his.

He groaned into his hands. Of course he couldn't do that. The lady had said no.

Shell felt his anger, his frustration, and part of her shared it. She knew what she'd done, and it was cruel. Men called women terrible names for less, but if she had known how it would be, how quickly her body would respond to him, how intense and almost inevitable the outcome of that kiss would be, she wouldn't have accepted it.

Would she? No! Never.

She bent and scooped up her sweater, then looked back at him. He had lifted his head and was staring at her, his eyes dark with questions for which she had no answers, questions he had every right to expect her to answer. What could she say? That she was sorry? He must know that. That she'd had to stop because if she hadn't, in another two minutes she'd be inviting a man she didn't know right into her bed?

He had to know that too. Just as he had to know that she couldn't do it!

Suddenly, an almost frightening anger surged in from nowhere, sending her reeling onto another emotional plane. It was anger with herself. Anger with Jase for making her feel this way. Anger with Lil for needing her so much. Anger with circumstances she had never been able to control. She welcomed the anger, husbanded it, let it grow strong enough to overcome the aching sense of loss. It rescued her from her overwhelming guilt, and she threw it at Jase as he came to his feet.

"No!" she said. "Stay away from me!"

Though he hadn't been approaching her, Jase stood rooted. She snatched up the flashlight. "I'll do what you want." Her voice broke as she whirled around and started across the room, her hair streaming down her naked back.

"What I want . . . ?" There was only one thing he wanted.

"I'll take you to my father's party." At the far side of the room, she turned back. Her sweater was crushed against her breasts, hiding them, and he had never been so aroused by the sight of a woman. Her eyes blazed into his. "You didn't have to try to seduce me, Jase. I'd have invited you anyway, if only to save my grandmother."

"Shell! Dammit, I wasn't—"

"Weren't you? I find that awfully hard to believe." She flicked an icy glance over him and turned away again.

"Good night," she said, and her inflection was as poisonous as if she'd said "Drop dead."

Several painful minutes later, Jase extinguished one lamp and, carrying the other, limped down the hall to his room. The oily stink of the lamp's dying smoke eradicated the feminine perfume that lingered too long in his mind.

All right, he told himself. Fine. It was just as well she'd called a halt to something that had been almost entirely out of hand. He didn't need involvement. He didn't want it. And he damned well wouldn't have it.

Not with Shirley Elizabeth Landry or anyone else!

"So there you are," Shell said when she finally found Jase the next morning. He stood beside the creek where Ned had the back end of a badly crumpled green Jeep hooked up to his tractor, preparing to haul it out of the now tame and shallow water. "Uh . . . hi."

Jase turned and looked at her, watching as she approached. For a long moment he said nothing, his eyes revealing no emotions. "Yup. Here I am," he said.

She lifted the cup she was carrying as in a toast. "Thanks for making the coffee. What time did the power come back on?"

"I don't know. When I got up, nearly every light in the house was blazing. I thought you were up."

And had left. He didn't say that, but she thought that was what he'd meant.

She managed a sketchy smile. "I should have checked switches, I guess, before I went to bed."

It had been a poor choice of words; she knew it as she said them. Their eyes met, held, and too many other, unspoken words crackled in the air between them. Shell clutched her coffee mug like a lifeline and forced herself to continue meeting his gaze. "Jase . . . I'm sorry. About last night."

He shrugged. "It's okay. My fault. I moved too fast. I'm sorry I scared you."

She drew a deep breath and shook her head. She owed him the truth, if nothing else. "You didn't scare me. *I* scared me."

For the first time since she'd come outside, he smiled. It was a slow, tender smile, full of gentle mockery, visible first as a lightening of his obsidian eyes, followed by an easing in the lines of tension in his face, then a curving of his lips. He took one long step that put him right in front of her, raised his arm, and rubbed the backs of his knuckles over her cheek. When he tucked her hair behind her left ear, she felt the touch right to the soles of her feet.

"*We* scared *us*," he said. "But sometimes things that are scary in the night aren't so threatening by the light of day."

She wasn't so sure of that. Simply being this close to him made her insides all loose and hot and needful. "Aren't they?"

He ran the broad pad of his thumb over her lips. "Do I make you feel threatened, Shell?"

Her awareness of herself, of her body, her heart, her lungs, her skin, was total. "A bit," she whispered. Staring into his eyes, she wished she knew him better, well enough to read him; wished he'd touch her hair again, or her lips. Her breasts or her aching nipples. What did a person do with this kind of wanting, except . . . ? She drew in a shuddering breath and held it. A smart person fought it until she knew where it was going.

This time his rough-edged finger outlined her ear. "What is it about me that scares you?"

All the things you can make me want, simply by being here, by looking at me, by touching me. Before she could find a way to articulate the emotions swelling and surging and roiling within, he asked softly, "Want to know what it is about you that scares me?"

She swallowed hard. "Sure, if you want to tell me."

"Your eyes, to start with. I'm afraid of drowning when I look into them." He brushed the tips of her lashes, and she closed her eyes. "And your mouth." He ran his thumb over her lower lip again. "It could capture me, hold me, make me crazy with wanting to kiss it." His hands encircled her waist, around the oversized sweatshirt she'd tugged on with her black leggings. "And your body." His cupped hands slid over her hips. "It could keep a man busy exploring its mysteries so long, he'd forget there were other . . . places he wanted to see."

She opened her eyes. He was smiling.

"I remember when we were children," she said. "You used to carve little boats out of driftwood and set them afloat with sails made of leaves. You told me they were going to China, and that someday you'd go there too. Did you?" *And did you meet a woman there, who became so important you still dream about her? A woman named Mai-Lee?*

He smiled widely. "You remember that?" She nodded. "I went there."

"And did a lot of . . . exploring?"

His hands tightened on her hips and he drew her closer. "Yes."

"Yet you still have exploring to do?"

"Lots more." His mouth stroked over her face and settled briefly under her chin, then he lifted his head. Brushing her hair back, he curved his hand around her nape. "Like I said, there's a lot of you I haven't seen yet."

Shell shuddered at the sensation his lips and fingers left behind, and burned with the need they engendered in her. She wouldn't think about Mai-Lee, or any other woman he might have known. He was thirty-three years old. Of course he'd known plenty of women. And she'd known a man or two as well.

"Lord," he breathed against her neck. "I could probably explore you and find things even *you* didn't know existed."

"That's . . . what scares me about you."

He lifted his head. "You don't have to be scared, Shell."

"But if you are," a man's voice intruded, "you know you need only to holler. Right, Shell?"

They both whirled, Jase more slowly than Shell, his hand trailing off her neck to rest on her shoulder. Ned was leaning against a tree trunk not three feet away, and Shell realized she had never seen him finish pulling the Jeep out of the creek bed, never heard him shut off the tractor, never been aware of his approach.

She glared at him. "Jase and I were having a private conversation, Ned."

"Pretty damned public place for a private talk, if you ask me."

"I don't recall doing so."

Ned shrugged. "Maybe not. Just remember, falling in love's like getting drunk. The first thing to go's the judgment."

Shell stared at him, her coffee mug dangling from one hand, dripping. Her "I'm not—" and Jase's "We aren't—" were overridden by Ned's snort, composed of equal parts derision and amusement. "How would you know? Like I said, judgment's the first thing to go.

"Now," he added briskly, "if you want a ride to work, and your buddy here wants to get into town to find somebody to haul this hunk of junk off our property, I suggest you go get ready. I'll be leaving in twenty minutes."

He turned and mounted his tractor, then roared away down the road toward home.

Neither Jase nor Shell moved for several moments. After the sound of the unmuffled engine had dwindled, the sudden and raucous call of a Steller's jay split the silence. Out over the ocean, gulls wheeled and mewed. Nearby, a squirrel executed a rapid spiral up a fir tree, barking a shrill warning as it ran.

Jase touched her cheek again. "You look as if you're about to run into the woods and hide."

She tried to smile, wanting to deny it. Was she that transparent? She *felt* as if she were about to run into the woods and hide. As if she should. Ned's words echoed in her mind. Falling in love . . . She wasn't! Of course she wasn't.

"I think we'll take it slow and easy from here on," Jase added. "That is, if there's going to be a 'from here on'?"

She searched his eyes. "I don't know."

"That's okay. Neither do I. But it would be nice to find out, wouldn't it?"

Slowly, reluctantly, she nodded. Her heart was beating so fast, it seemed ready to explode. She didn't know if it was from excitement or fear. "It would . . . be nice." Yet the idea was fraught with terror for her. Obstacles. So many obstacles! Two totally different lives. Two totally different geographical locations. He wasn't a country person—she knew that from things he'd said the day before—and she was. More, she had to live where she did. She had no choice. Lil needed her, and Lil had to be here. Lil also had to come first. Shell wanted to weep. And yes, she wanted to run away and hide, as she had as a little girl when the reporters and fans had screamed their incessant questions, popped their myriad flashbulbs, reached with their impatient, grasping hands. But . . .

She squared her shoulders. She was an adult, for heaven's sake. If there were difficulties ahead, she could face them. She would deal with them. She would meet each one as it occurred and beat it down.

Jase laughed softly and slid his fingers into her hair, but only for a moment. He snatched his hand away and stuffed it into the back pocket of his jeans. "I think that's exactly the way you'd look as the firing squad took aim at your heart."

"Is it?" It wasn't a firing squad she was worried about. There was that little fat pink guy with his bow and arrow, and she suspected he might be sitting somewhere in the branches of the trees at her back. It was time to get out of there, to get to work in her store and let reality take over her life again.

Whatever this was, lust maybe, a crush at best, she couldn't allow it to dominate her thoughts. She wasn't going to fall in love with a man she didn't know. Love took a long time to develop. It grew between two people who had known each other for months, even years.

It didn't spring into full being in thirty-six hours.

Still, when Jase linked their fingers together and turned her toward the road, she didn't pull away. The feel of their two palms together, their fingers entwined, was a pleasure she refused to deny herself. It, at least, was an innocuous pleasure, a reassuringly safe one, one she was sure wouldn't lead to something she couldn't handle.

"Very nice." Jase stood in the main aisle of Shell's store and looked around, his hands in the pockets of his water-stained suede jacket, the overhead lights bouncing a sheen off his hair. He riffled a hand through a stack of paperback romances on a spinning rack, gave the rack a gentle nudge, and slid his gaze down the new row exposed by its rotation. Next, he checked out a wooden pagoda filled with rows of science fiction and fantasy books, then circled it to scan the titles of several historical tomes.

Farther into the store, he bent and hefted a large leather-bound Bible, holding it to his nose. "Bookstores always smell nice."

Shell thought he looked out of place in her quiet little shop. He was too large, too vital, too forceful, as if he'd be too busy having adventures himself to ever sit down and read about other people having them. He was too intent on exploring.

She strode quickly away from him before her mind got caught up thinking about his doing more "exploring" of her body.

He followed her toward the front of the store. "This is a great bookstore," he said. "I like it."

"What do you like about it?" She slid open the main doors to the mall, letting in the sound of Roger Whittaker singing "Past Three O'clock."

Jase had to smile at the faint anxiety he heard in Shell's voice, touched that she wanted him to approve. And he did. "It's a warm place," he said without hesitation. "Very welcoming."

The walls, as much as could be seen above the well-filled dark walnut bookshelves, were painted a restful peach. Above the travel section posters of places as diverse as Greece, Niagara Falls, and Rio surrounded a huge world map. He could picture Shell teetering on a stepladder, snapping in staples to hold the posters.

A three-foot-long set of wooden salad servers hung suspended above the cookbook section, and the books on nature were marked by various stuffed animals dangling on invisible strings from the ceiling, including a starfish and a giant prawn. The location of gardening books was indicated by an outsized rake-and-hoe set, carved from the same-type wood as the salad servers. The whimsy of it pleased him and told him more about her than he'd known from seeing her home.

The store, too, was as much a spot for friends to meet as it was a place of business. Throughout the store, wicker chairs provided places for browsers to sit and flip through books, or just to chat. A small table near the back had six little chairs shoved under it and a stack of well-worn books spread across it. Beside that, colorful wooden and plastic toys spilled from a well-stocked toybox. Obviously, she liked children and went out of her way to make them welcome.

The windows were a further revelation. A manger scene filled one, beautifully arranged with carved figures and a star that twinkled brightly when she switched on a spotlight. The other window held a selection of cookbooks, each with a cover featuring a festive meal. They were flanked by several oversized storybooks opened to illustrations of families surrounding their tree, or reading by a fireside, or playing together. Family, Jase mused. Oh, yes, she knew what that was all about. He sighed. He didn't.

Three women came in, one pushing a stroller and leading a small girl. The girl ran as if completely at home to the book table in the children's corner. A pair of laughing teenage boys jostled each other as they roughhoused through the door, then steadied up to let an elderly man with a walker pass between them. The telephone rang, and Shell darted behind the counter to pick it up, saying briskly, "Good morning. Legacy." Behind her, a fax machine hummed to life and pinged an electronic note, sending a sheet of paper fluttering into the basket. As she talked, she picked it up and scanned it. Setting it down, she leaned over and switched on a computer that stood opposite the cash register.

Jase watched and listened as Shell's workday began, warmed up, and started to hum in high gear. He sank into one of the gaily cushioned wicker chairs near her cash desk, sighing as he leaned back.

A secret part of him that he'd scarcely known existed mourned the intrusion of the modern world, regretted the silent closing of the small time warp he'd slipped through to find a miracle in the night.

"Legacy," he said to Shell an hour later, when there was a lull between Christmas shoppers. "Why did you name your store Legacy? Because you bought it with one?"

She laughed. She was perched on the stool behind the counter, flipping through the pages of a microfiche that sped across the screen in a dizzying blue-and-white blur. "Good heavens, no." She stopped the whirling print, made a notation on paper, and went on. "The full name of the store is Gutenberg's Legacy."

Jase shook his head, not getting it for a moment, then he laughed. "Very good. If it hadn't been for Gutenberg . . ."

"That's right." She slipped another fiche into

the reader and whizzed through it until she found what she wanted. He wondered if she had a listing for *When Angels Fall* by Jason Calhoun, and thought of asking her but held his words back. There would be a time and a place to discuss that, and this was not it.

"Every time I see a mass-produced book," she continued, shutting down the microfiche viewer, "I mentally thank him for his movable type. I thought it only right that he be honored."

Another crowd of shoppers came in then, and it wasn't until Shell's assistant, Carrie, arrived to relieve her at lunchtime that Jase had an opportunity to talk to her again.

Dipping into his big bowl of clam chowder in a restaurant near the mall, he said, "Your store looks very successful. You must be proud."

"It's coming along." The brilliance of her smile and the eager light in her eyes belied her modesty. "The first couple of years were dicey, but I'm holding my own now, managing not only to pay the rent and buy stock, but pay down the principal on the mortgage."

Mortgage? he repeated silently. The daughter of Elwin Landry had a mortgage?

Jase realized he was staring at her, his mouth half-open. He closed it and bit back the impulse to ask why her father hadn't helped her financially. His face heated uncomfortably when her light laugh told him she'd all-too-accurately read his mind.

"Really, Jase! Did you think Gutenberg's Legacy was a toy my rich daddy had bought for me to play with?"

"I . . . well . . ." He crumbled a cracker into his chowder, frowning down at his hands.

Shell had to laugh again at Jase's obvious discomfort. Clearly, she'd been right on the mark. He looked up, contrite but confused. She let him off the hook.

"Sorry to disappoint you, but I've done it all on my own, by choice. I've saved like Scrooge, cutting corners wherever I could, wearing the same clothes for season after season, taking very little personal pay so I could pay back my business loan, just like regular folks. I wanted to prove to myself and anybody else who doubted me that I could do it."

Something in her tone prompted him to ask, "Who else might have doubted you?"

Her mouth twisted. "My father, for one." She ate half a slice of toast, then licked her lips before patting them with her napkin. It made Jase's own lips tingle as he watched her. "As soon as he knew I wanted a bookstore," she went on, "he was all for buying me one. But he'd have also bought me a manager to run the place and hired a pile of accountants to make sure his money was well spent and that I was in no danger of wasting it. I wanted it to be mine."

She tilted up her chin. "*All* mine. So I did it alone."

"Good for you. It can't have been easy."

It hadn't been, and she was grateful to him for recognizing that. Tears stung her eyes, and she had to blink rapidly and look away from him. Dammit, what was the matter with her? Why was Jase's approval so important to her?

It wasn't, of course. It was simply that it was nice to have her hard work acknowledged. She took another bite of her thick, ham-laden pea soup and forced herself to glance up at him again. "Of course, I pay very low rent for my home, and that helped a lot, as did the fact that I have . . . uh, well, expectations. Bank managers find that . . . comforting."

Jase reached across the table and touched the back of her hand. He slid his fingers the length of hers, lingering for a moment on her nails, then repeated the gesture. "I'm sure you got your loan because you had a sound business proposition to show them. I don't suppose 'expectations' would carry much weight, since your parents aren't exactly ready for the nursing home."

She picked up a crumb from her toast and dropped it back onto her plate, purely to regain control of her hand.

She couldn't think, couldn't reason, while he touched her.

Should she tell him? Would it make a difference? It was one thing to be thought of as an heiress who wouldn't inherit for many years. It was another to be known as a woman of not inconsiderable means in her own right. She liked Jase. She knew she could learn, and quickly, to more than merely like him. It was his feelings that kept her off balance—or, more accurately, her not knowing what his feelings were. He wanted her. There was no way she could pretend not to know that. But how much more would he want her if he knew?

Instinct told her that Jase O'Keefe was not like that. But could instincts always be trusted? Drawing in a deep breath, she met his gaze and took an enormous leap of faith.

Eight

"When I first applied for a business loan," she said, "I kept my father's identity and his connection with commercial banking completely out of the picture. But I did have one thing to use as collateral, and I used it." She smiled as if Jase's reaction, whatever it might be, was immaterial to her. "You see, I'm due to come into a substantial trust from my grandfather's estate when I turn thirty, so the bank knew it wouldn't have to wait too long if my store didn't make it and I defaulted."

She saw Jase swallow. "So," he said, his tone flat. "You're a rich woman. Or you will be."

"You sound . . . disappointed." That wasn't what she'd expected. She was accustomed to a different reaction from men—the kind of men her father liked to send across her path.

"I think I am."

A thought occurred to her. "Disappointed in

what? That I'm going to have money, or that I don't have it yet?"

His gaze narrowed. "I believe I've just been insulted."

She cringed. "I'm sorry."

He relented. "I like money as much as the next guy, Shell, but I'd never go after a woman simply because she had it."

She wet her lips. "Or turn away from one—simply because she did?"

He let out a long breath. "It can't help but change things."

She looked down at the table. "I know."

After a moment he reached over and tilted up her chin. "Hey, we were going to take things slow and easy, weren't we? Just sort of relax and see what comes. Why don't we do that about this too? After all, your birthday's not for a couple of months, and that can be a long, long time."

In a relationship? she wanted to ask. *Do your relationships usually last less than that?* She didn't ask, only nodded. Anyway, they didn't have a relationship, did they? They had little more than some shared kisses, a mutual desire, and a problem to solve together. When that was done, he'd go back to his own life. The one he'd said he wanted to "get on with" once he'd taken care of the man who had harmed his grandmother.

"Why thirty?" he asked, drawing her attention back to the here and now. "Why not twenty-one, or eighteen? That's the age of majority here, isn't it?"

"Yes, but Grandpa was old-fashioned about women. My brothers get their inheritances when they turn twenty-one, but Grandpa had no faith in any woman's ability to look after her own affairs."

"Your grandmother?" A look of mingled hope and dismay crossed his face. "Did he arrange for someone else to—"

Shell shook her head. "No. Her, he trusted. But, of course, that was because he'd spent many years teaching her the 'right' way to do things. As for me, he was certain that by the time I turned thirty, I'd be safely married to some fine, upstanding fellow, preferably of my father's choosing, and *he*, the husband, could take over my money and make sure I didn't do anything foolish with it."

Jase laughed suddenly. "And do you plan to do it that way?"

"What, spend my inheritance foolishly?" To her amazement, she felt light and silly, as if telling him about her money had freed her in some way. "Absolutely. Wanna help?"

"Can't think of anything more fun," he said, "but what I was talking about was your marrying some guy of your father's choosing."

She laughed too. "I do not. Not that he believes it, of course. That's what the Christmas party's all about, really, every year. I only go to check out his annual parade of suitors. From them I accept only three to, as Dad puts it, 'give a fighting chance.' If it weren't for my agreement with him, I wouldn't bother going at all."

Jase looked at her laughing face, not quite sure if he should believe her. He remembered the mercurial, elfin humor she'd evinced even as a little girl. "I see. You have an agreement with your dad regarding suitors. What does that entail?"

Was Elwin's approval required if a guy wanted to become a suitor? Jase wondered. He didn't ask, though. He refused to ask. He'd long ago quit seeking approval from anyone. But to his dismay, he found himself wishing he'd spent more time learning about Elwin Landry and what might please him, what might not.

He drew himself up short. "Suitor" was not a term he'd ever apply to himself. It suggested a permanence he no longer sought in a relationship.

". . . as long as I accept three of his candidates at the party," Shell was saying when he picked up the conversation again, "and give each of them a minimum of one date afterward, he stops tossing men across my path for the rest of the year."

Her eyes gleamed like emeralds in sunlight. "I can't wait to see how he reacts when he sees me walking in with a date. Of my own choosing."

Jase's breath caught in his throat. Was that how she saw him? As a date "of her own choosing"? Before he started dwelling on how much that meant to him, and why, he asked, "How does he go about throwing men across your path with you living where you do?"

"He doesn't do that anymore. That's what the agreement's all about. Before we made our pact, he'd invite me to lunch—just us, he'd assure me—then, at the last minute, some young businessman from out of town, who just happened to be at loose ends, would join us. Then Dad would be 'called away,' leaving me to entertain his friend."

She made a face. "Honestly, he kept bombarding me with the most unlikely types. Of course, he thought they were very likely."

"Such as?"

"Let's see." She ate the last of her soup, then shoved her bowl away and pulled her coffee cup nearer. "The last year I let him get away with that, before I came back here and opened my store, his selection included a bombastic little fellow with dandruff and a highly inflated opinion of his own value, but he had an MBA from Harvard, so Dad approved. Another one looked good to Dad because he was a lawyer, but what Dad overlooked was the guy's utterly disgusting habit of sniffing with every third word he spoke. But the worst one he ever saddled me with was a newspaperman."

Jase winced. Right. He remembered her explosive reaction when he'd mentioned having seen her picture in the paper. He clenched his hands under the table. "And you hate newsmen." It wasn't a question.

Her eyes flared, green sparked with golden lights. "There's no lower scum on earth than people who make their living off other people's grief or misfortune, who scrape up dirt and spread it around, creating the illusion of filth even where none exists!"

"Not all newspaper writers do that."

She raised one skeptical brow. "Give any one of them a chance and that's exactly what he'll do. And then he'll use the excuse that the public buys papers only to read bad news, that it sells better than good news. That," she added, shoving back her chair and getting to her feet, "is one of the reasons I seldom look at newspapers. I don't need my life filled with that kind of garbage."

Jase took his still-soggy wallet from his pocket, peeled apart a couple of soaked bills, and tossed them onto the table. "What about current affairs? Isn't ignoring the news sort of like hiding your head in the sand? Or maybe like living in a time warp?"

She flicked a glance over him, as she headed toward the exit. "Not at all. I'm pretty well up on what goes on in the world. I just avoid sleaze and the people who produce it. As well as the places it's published, and that includes daily papers."

"Shell—" he began. He was interrupted by a man who recognized Shell and wanted to know if the book he'd ordered was in yet. When that man had passed on by, it was one friend or neighbor or customer after another all the way back to the mall. When they reached her store, Carrie told Jase that the garage had called and wanted him to drop by as soon as possible. A loaner car was available for him now.

"Later?" he asked Shell, searching her eyes as he held her arm, preventing her from helping a customer for just a moment. "Dinner?"

She shook her head. "Ned's picking me up right after work. I don't want to ask him to make two trips, Jase."

"I'll come get you myself. Please, Shell?" He'd booked a room in a hotel on the way to the store that morning.

Shell shook her head. She needed a time-out from him, so she could sort through all the different emotions he'd aroused in her, all the different things he'd made her think about, the different questions he had her asking herself.

"Jase, please, don't ask."

He traced the line of her chin. "Okay," he said as if he understood what she needed, and why. "But don't let Ned drive you to work tomorrow. I'll pick you up on this side of the washout, and we'll have breakfast together, all right?"

Shell thought of the suitcase she'd be carrying tomorrow, in order to leave right after closing time to catch the ferry into the city for her father's party.

With Jase.

Her heart tripped, and before she could prevent it, she'd reached up and smoothed back the thick, crisp hair that persisted in falling over his forehead.

"Tomorrow," she said. "For breakfast."

Never before had the thought of breakfast with a man given her what she was sure would be a terminal case of butterflies.

Get through the day, she told herself. Get through the night. And let tomorrow happen. . . .

"You look as if you belong on the top of that Christmas tree," Jase said, sliding his arm around Shell as the band began playing a slow, old-fashioned tune. Even with his sore leg, he thought he could dance to this one. For the past hour he'd had to watch as a succession of what he assumed were potential suitors beat out a rhythm with Shell on the highly polished floor of the conservatory in her father's Point Gray home.

That had beat out a rhythm within him, a deep, dark, primitive one that had him clenching his fists and teeth as he watched. She'd returned to his side frequently, only to be drawn away by another swain. At last he had her all to himself, and until his leg gave out, he didn't mean to let her go.

Dressed in a gold lamé gown that left her shoulders bare and clung to her body from breast to hip before flaring out in a crinoline-stiffened bell that ended just above her knees, she looked more beautiful than he'd dreamed she would. His only regret was that instead of leaving her hair loose, she'd swept it up and fastened it to the back of her head with a glittering gold clip.

She smiled up at him. "And you look as if you belong in an elegant ballroom. I'm darned sure you didn't have a tuxedo hidden away in that beat-up old tote bag of yours. How did you manage a rental on such short notice?"

He twirled her away, then held her at arm's length as he stroked one hand down his lapel. "Now does this fit like a rented suit?"

She grinned. "Looking for compliments?"

"Of course."

"It fits," she said as he spun her around again and brought her up against his chest, "like it was made for you." She ran her hand up his chest and around to the back of his neck.

Jase shuddered in pleasure. For a moment he couldn't resist resting his cheek on her hair as they danced behind a tall banana plant, whose fronds brushed the glass roof overhead. Oh, Lord, but she smelled good. He wished he could spirit her away, take her with him back to his hotel when this evening was over, instead of leaving her with her family.

"It *was* made for me," he said, forcing himself to concentrate on the conversation. "Yesterday, while I waited for you to get off work, I called a friend in L.A. He burgled my apartment and sent it up by courier to my hotel."

She tilted her head back. "Your coming without your tuxedo indicates a certain lack of confidence completely unexpected in a man of your . . . um, talents."

He swung her past a grouping of wicker chairs and glass tables, where several couples sat sipping champagne. "My 'talents'?" he asked, grinning down at her. "Believe me, little Shell, you haven't begun to learn about my talents."

He loved the lively color that spread over her cheeks and made her eyes glitter. He loved, too, the way she lowered her lashes for just an instant, then widened her eyes and looked up at him with exaggerated innocence. She was flirting with him, and it delighted him to catch her in this mood.

"Maybe I know all I care to know about those talents," she said.

He tightened his arm around her waist. "And maybe you don't."

She smiled, ducked her head, and for just an instant rested her brow against his shirtfront. "Maybe," she conceded, then returned the conversation to his sending for his tux.

"Would you have me believe that you didn't bring evening dress with you because you weren't completely certain you'd be able to persuade me to get you into this bash?"

His smile faded, and he shook his head. "Until I arrived here, Shell, I didn't know you were connected to the people I had to meet, had no idea I'd be seeing an old childhood friend." He drew her closer. "Or dancing with her in Elwin Landry's conservatory."

She had forgotten that. Amazing, she mused. It sometimes seemed that the two of them had been together forever, instead of merely four days; that she hadn't let his memory lie dormant in the back of her mind until he awakened it with a reminder of a mouthful of live crabs.

As he held Shell and swayed to the music, Jase glanced at her father. Elwin Landry was tall and rawboned, with a face that made Jase think of Abraham Lincoln despite his Nordic coloring. They had met at dinner, and Jase had been taken at once by the older man's quick intelligence and wide knowledge not only of finances, but of other world affairs. Jase wondered how a man of Elwin's caliber could maintain the outmoded belief that his daughter needed someone to make her decisions for her.

His wife, Sondra, was small and vivacious, her hands constantly in motion, touching, patting, gesturing. While she appeared to be brainless and fluffy, with her froth of strawberry-blond curls more suited to a girl of twenty than a woman of fifty, Jase had discovered in her a mind as incisive as her husband's. Elwin appeared to have no trouble accepting his wife as his equal. So why did he want to choose his daughter's mate?

"How do you think your father took it," he asked Shell, "your bringing me along? The man certainly has a knack for hiding what he feels."

"I think Dad likes you," she said. "At least he hasn't put you through the third degree, the way he used to with the men I dated while I was in college."

"Maybe he's beginning to trust your judgment."

Shell looked down, remembering Ned's warning that the first thing to go was one's judgment. She was more than a little afraid he might be right. From the moment she and Jase had met that morning, and all through the day, she'd been more and more certain that she was in danger of losing her head over, as well as her heart to, the man.

Yet what could she do? How could she protect herself against herself? And did she really want to? Even if their relationship was to be brief, should she deny herself the joy it would bring?

The music blended from one big-band-era piece into another, and yet another, and she nestled close to Jase. She was achingly aware of his scent, his power, his tenderness whenever he touched her face or curved a hand over her shoulder. Sometimes he swung her away so he could look at her, smile at her, but always, every time, he gathered her back close to him with what sounded like a gentle groan of pleasure. It was a pleasure she shared to the full depths of her being, a pleasure she wished would never end.

When another couple brushed too close and he tried to swing Shell aside, his leg gave way. He stumbled and took a quick step sideways to catch himself against a papa-san chair.

"Sorry about that," he murmured. He tried to draw her back into his arms, but she shook her head and stepped away, holding out one hand.

"Your leg," she said. "It's had enough, hasn't it? Come on, there's something I want to show you anyway."

He laughed, drawing more than one glance toward him, glances that lingered enviously as he linked his fingers with Shell's and grinned irrepressibly at her. "Women have etchings now?" he asked.

She laughed. "That," she said, "comes later."

He held her close to his side and smiled into her eyes. But his smile faded and his voice was husky as he asked, "Promise?"

Before she could swallow the tightness in her throat and form a reply, the butler stopped a respectful distance in front of her and cleared his throat.

The butler—Jase had been more than just a little taken aback to learn that the Landry family had a real butler—gave a little bow. "Miss Landry, your grandmother and Mr. Graves have just arrived. You asked to be informed."

"Thank you, Whittier," Shell said, and the man bowed again and disappeared.

Shell looked at Jase, her eyes wide with worry and anxiety.

"Sweetheart . . ." He wished he had never involved her in this. He hated what it was doing to her, and he abandoned his plan of having her introduce him to Sterling. "Listen. I've been thinking. Your grandmother doesn't have to know you and I are . . . connected in any way. I'll simply stay away from you. She won't notice another strange face in this mob, and as soon as Sterling has a drink, I'll find a way to get the glass, then I'll leave unobtrusively. There's no reason for you to be involved."

"I have to be involved." Her gaze, her voice, were resolute. "For one thing, I haven't shown you yet where I stashed your equipment. And if you aren't wrong, then Grandma's going to need me."

She faltered for just a moment. "Oh, Lord, Jase, I hope you are wrong! I don't want to see my grandmother hurt."

Briefly cupping her cheek, he offered what comfort he could in such a public setting. "I know. And maybe I am wrong."

He wasn't. The moment he saw Sterling Graves, his head thrown back, laughing as he clapped Elwin on the shoulder, Jase knew he had his man. He didn't need fingerprints to satisfy him. He would get them though, if only to satisfy Shell. And her grandmother.

The introductions went smoothly enough, except for one touchy moment when Sterling gave him a sharper look than was required. Jase had known all along Sterling might say something like "Have we met?" or "I seem to know your face." It wouldn't have surprised Jase, nor would it have fazed him. He had his reply ready. Apart from that momentary narrowing of his eyes, though, Sterling said nothing.

Maybe Sterling was like Shell, Jase thought, and didn't read the daily newspapers.

• • •

"Got it," he said to Shell half an hour later. He was carrying Sterling's glass gingerly, trying to look casual, as if he were on the way to the bar for a refill.

"All right," she said. She slipped her arm through his and led him through the throng. "In here." They had slipped out of the main reception area and into a corridor, and she opened a heavy door, gesturing him in.

They passed through a library with walls of books that looked as if they had been read often over the years, but she didn't stop there. She led him past a fireplace with logs laid ready for lighting, past several leather sofas and chairs, to a locked door.

"This is Dad's office," she said as she unlocked and opened the door. "You can use that table for whatever you have to do, and there's the fax machine you said you'd need." She opened the bottom drawer of an oak filing cabinet. "I stored the things you asked me to smuggle in, in here."

Then, as if she couldn't bear to watch him, she spun on the spike heel of a gold sandal and strode to an embrasured window, well outside the pool of light from the one lamp she'd turned on for him. When he was done, he switched off the lamp and came up behind her. She was watching a parade of brightly decorated boats glide by along the shore of Point Gray.

"Carol ships," she said as he slid his arms around her waist, drawing her back against his chest. "Look, Jase. Aren't they beautiful?"

"Very beautiful," he said. The boats came in a steady stream, in every size from cruise ships to runabouts, and each one celebrated Christmas. There were sailboats with Santa's sleigh and reindeer dancing up through the rigging, power boats with fully adorned trees on their cabin roofs, and others merely outlined in bright colored lights.

"I love to see them." Shell's voice wobbled, but she went on. "If we were outside, we could hear the music they broadcast. Thousands of people line the shores of False Creek, English Bay, and Burrard Inlet to see and hear the ships every year, regardless of the weather. They sail most weekends through December. People pay to ride on the bigger boats, have dinner parties aboard, while others are small family groups, even individuals who just want to be part of the scene. They—" Her voice cracked, breaking on a sob, and she spun around and dug her fingers into his biceps. "Dammit, Jase, how long will we have to wait?"

He hugged her, rocking her from side to side. "It shouldn't be much longer."

She let out a ragged sigh, and he tucked her head under his chin, wishing she didn't have to go through this agony of waiting. He wished he didn't have to go through the agony of holding her and not obeying his instincts, but she wouldn't want that from him right now. All she wanted from him was reassurance that her grandmother's life was not about to be shattered, and that was something he couldn't give her.

"Jase . . ." She lifted her head and looked up at him. After a moment's hesitation she slid her hands up around the back of his neck, pulled his head down, and kissed him. With a shudder of need he wrapped her in a deep embrace and parted her lips with his tongue.

When he lifted his head, moments later, she let out a tremulous sigh and traced the outline of his mouth with one fingertip. He caught it, sucked on it, and felt her shiver. "When you kiss me," she whispered, "I forget everything. That's one talent of yours I'm beginning to know quite well."

He smiled. Linking his hands at the small of her back, he leaned against a mullion and drew her in between his legs. "Too well?"

She shook her head. "I don't think kissing is something that can be overdone."

"Well, certainly not when you and I are doing it," he murmured, and took her lips again, thrusting deep with his tongue, dipping and stroking and teasing until she moaned and went heavy in his arms, as if she wanted to lie down. He trailed his mouth across her face, down her neck, over her shoulders, then back to her lips. She rose up on tiptoe, straining against him, pressing close, moving in a rhythm that pounded through him like heavy, throbbing music.

"Oh, Lord, sweetheart, stop," he said, tearing his mouth away and holding her back from him.

"Stop? Why?" She slid a hand inside his jacket and placed it unerringly over his heart. Her fingers toyed with his hard nipple, rotating it; then she raked over it with a thumbnail. "I like to feel you go as wild as you make me."

He liked it too. "But if we don't cut this out, things are going to escalate, and . . ."

"And . . ." She nipped the skin of his neck with her teeth, then kissed away the sting.

He groaned. "And I'm going to give in to temptation and do . . . this." He unzipped her dress, folded it down, and stroked his tongue over one of her nipples.

"Ahhh!" It was a cry of pure ecstasy as she arched to his mouth. "Jase!" Her hips rocked against him as he tugged, sucking the nipple deep into his mouth. He took her hand and placed it over his hardness, and after a moment's hesitation she curled her fingers around him while he licked and suckled her other nipple.

Her hand tightened, moving in an erotic rhythm, and it was his turn to shudder and whisper her name. He backed up to a leather couch that stood facing the window embrasure, carrying her with him, then sank down, pulling her astride his lap. He held her tightly, his hips pumping insistently as he palmed her breasts and kissed her deeply, again and again, until his head spun and she clung weakly to him, whispering his name like a plea.

He rested his head on her shoulder, arching his neck to the delicious sensation of her hands in his hair. When she leaned back, urging his mouth to her breasts again, he shook his head. "We . . . have . . . to stop," he gasped. He slid her onto the cushions beside him but couldn't resist bending to kiss her breasts again, lingering on each nipple before sitting up. "Hide those luscious breasts, my darling, or I won't be responsible for my actions."

She groaned, then laughed unsteadily. "You're

the one who exposed them." She pulled her dress back up and turned so he could zip it. "Lord, Jase! I can't believe we did that. In my father's office. Without locking the door."

He kissed the back of her neck before spinning her around to face him. He buried his face for a moment in her cleavage, then looked at her again.

"I only did it because your breasts have been tempting me all evening, ever since I arrived for dinner and realized you couldn't possibly be wearing a bra under that dress." He laughed. "Oh, what am I saying? All evening? Hell!"

Getting to his feet, he returned to the window and looked out, wondering how long it would take him to lose his erection this time. He turned back to her. "Since the moment I woke up with your hands on my thigh," he said, "I've been in a constant state of arousal."

"I'm sorry. . . ." It sounded, he thought, as if she were asking if she should be.

And she should not. He drew a deep breath, seeking calmness. It didn't help. Returning to her, he crouched before her, his hands on the cushions by her hips, not touching, not daring to touch. "Shell—" He sounded breathless, like a randy kid about to ask a girl for the first time if she'd come and park with him on a lovers' lane. "Do—do you have to stay here tonight? With your folks?"

"Jase . . . I . . ." He heard her swallow. "No," she whispered. "No. I don't have to."

He went weak with desire. "Come back with me," he said jerkily. "To my hotel. I want you, Shell, and I think you want me."

She leaned back as if she had gone weak, as weak as he felt. "You *think*?"

He laughed. Was she saying yes? "All right, I know. But I don't know if you're willing to give in to that . . . desire. Are you? Will you? Can—"

"Sterling," a man's voice sounded from the library, "you must be mistaken. Shell would never entertain a newsman. In my home or anywhere else. She hates them. It's almost pathological with her! He said at dinner he works for the U.S. government. The IRS."

Shell twisted around on the couch as her father entered the dark office with Sterling Graves. "Wha—" she whispered, then broke off as Jase's hand wrapped tightly around her upper arm, silencing her.

Nine

"The IRS be damned!" Sterling exclaimed, his voice quavering with indignation. "The minute we were introduced, I knew I'd seen that face somewhere. I may be old, but I'm not senile, and it took me a while, but I remembered where I'd seen him. On page six of the *Los Angeles Echo*. On Mondays, Wednesdays, and Fridays. I tell you, Elwin, the man's a reporter, and I felt you should be warned, that Shell's dear mother should be warned."

"Lil has met the man." Elwin's own voice was curt. "If he were what you suspect, don't you think the secret would be out by now?"

Secret? Shell wondered. What secret? Then the conversation began to make sense, and she snatched her arm out of Jase's hold, fighting for breath, for words.

"However," her father went on, "the matter can be cleared up in short order." He switched on a light. "I'll simply ask the *Echo* to fax me a picture of— Why Shell! What are you two doing in here?"

"Snooping, no doubt," said Sterling, sweeping an accusing glare over both her and Jase. "Maybe helping her reporter boyfriend find whatever it is he came for."

"Reporter?" Shell finally found her voice and whirled out from behind the sofa to confront Sterling. "You're crazy! Jase is no such thing. He's—"

"A reporter for the *Los Angeles Echo*," Jase said smoothly. At that moment the fax machine gave its two distinctive rings. He walked over to it, picked up the paper as it rolled into the basket, scanned it, then folded it and slid it into his inside jacket pocket.

"May I ask what that was?" Elwin asked coolly, anger underlying his tone.

"Personal business," Jase said, just as coolly. "Shell offered me the use of your machine." He turned to Sterling.

"I see you've recognized me."

Shell stared at Jase, feeling faint.

"Has he." Neither Elwin's tone nor expression betrayed his emotions. He flicked a glance at Shell and took a step toward her. She stiffened and kept her gaze pinned on Jase's face as he answered her father.

"Yes, sir. I write a thrice-weekly column for the *Echo*."

No, no, no! Something in Shell sobbed like a beaten guitar.

"A thrice-weekly *gossip* column," Sterling put in with a sneer, his normally laughing blue eyes as icy as a Winnipeg winter. "He finds weak spots in celebrities, politicians, anyone, and exploits them. He makes even the strong vulnerable, because if he can't find an opening, a chink in a man's armor, he creates one by insinuation and foul innuendo, then pounces and devours his prey. He's a jackal."

Shell found her voice at last, but it was ragged, hoarse. "Jase! Tell Dad why you're here." Inwardly, she begged him, *And tell me none of this is true!*

He smiled. "Your father knows why I'm here, Shell. Sterling told him. He's quite correct. I work for the *Los Angeles Echo*. I'm after a story."

Her eyes burned. Pain ran up the back of her neck into her head. "A story? About my father?"

He shrugged negligently. "A man can't be as simon-pure as your father makes out he is. If he and his bank weren't part of the money-laundering scheme, how did he know so much about it? Somebody here tonight has the answer to that, Shell, and I intended to find it. If not at this party, then later, through contacts I'd hoped to make while you were busy entertaining your potential suitors. I only regret that it didn't work out that way."

She backed away from him, feeling sick. He wasn't going to quit fooling around and explain things to her father. He wasn't going to turn on Sterling and call him a liar.

He couldn't. Because *he* was the liar. He had lied to her. All along. About everything!

Her mind reeled. And she had exposed her mother to him? Exposed her father? Though she knew he'd never find anything true to write about that could harm Elwin, what if, as Sterling said, he printed just enough innuendo to ruin what was becoming an illustrious, internationally respected career that could well end up with an ambassadorship?

And Lilianne! Enough had been said to put him on the track, to suggest to a man with the kind of mind he must have that there was a secret to be dug out. Looking at him, at his complacent face, she knew that he had used her, had done what she'd accused him of doing his second night in her home—seduced her for his own purposes, none of which had to do with caring or wanting or even liking her. She'd been nothing more than a tool.

"Oh, God, Jase!" The words came out as a low, aching moan. "How could you do this to me?" She caught the back of the couch in her hands, her fingers biting into the rich leather.

He met her gaze, shrugged, and grinned—like a jackal. "Hell, Shirl. A man's gotta do what a man's gotta do."

She stared at him in total disbelief. *A man's gotta do what . . .*

Her heart turned over with a terrible lurch as she remembered another time he had said that to her. She had laughingly called him a hero, and he had said she should see him in action when she was in peril. He had called her Pauline. And now, he had called her not Shell, as he always did, but Shirl, as her mother did.

She continued to stare at him, then took another enormous leap of faith, faith in her own instincts, faith in the man, faith in the future. To conceal it, she whirled away from him contemptuously.

"He hasn't learned a damned thing here tonight, Daddy. I can promise you that. He's been too busy trying to seduce me. I'm happy to report that he didn't succeed in that, either. I suggest you call security and have him thrown out. Now, if you two gentlemen"— she deliberately refrained from looking at Jase and including him in the honorific— "will excuse me, I'm going to my room."

Elwin gazed at her with sympathy. "Shell, honey, I—"

She stood on tiptoe and kissed her father's cheek. "I'll be all right, Dad. But I want to be alone for a while. Please make my excuses, and give Sondra my apologies. Just get rid of that—that scum for me."

She wheeled and strode out, head held high.

An hour later Shell knocked at the door of Jase's hotel room. He opened it, dragged her in, and slammed the door shut. Leaning against it, he held her tight and kissed her until she was limp and he was not.

"Really!" She arched away from him. "'A man's gotta do what a man's gotta do'? Jase! What kind of real writer would use a phrase like that?"

"One who writes a column purely as a cover," he said. "As a reason for being in the Los Angeles area and for visiting Palm Springs, where most of my 'victims' reside. I have to appear to be gainfully employed. Hell, since I took my leave of absence, I've had to *be* gainfully employed."

He hugged her tightly again. "Thank you for being quick enough to pick up on my message." He swallowed visibly. "And thank you for coming here."

She placed her hands on his face and captured his gaze with her own. "I was invited, wasn't I?"

He drew in a deep breath. As he released it, it fanned across her cheek, lifting tiny tendrils of hair that had escaped her French roll when she'd dragged a sweatshirt over her head. "Darling, you don't need an invitation. Ever."

She closed her eyes and smiled. He kissed her lids, her lips, her chin, then she turned her face away. He looked at her questioningly.

"I have to know," she said. "Do you . . . do what he said, Jase?"

He undid the clip at the back of her head, slowly worked her hair loose, and spread it over her shoulders. "Find weak spots?"

She nodded.

"Yes," he said, his tone hard, his eyes momentarily cold. "When someone needs to have his deeds exposed and I can get the goods on him, I do it. But create them where they don't exist? No. I never have. I never will."

She shrugged out of her jacket, letting it fall to the floor. "I'm sorry I had to ask."

He stripped off her sweatshirt, then cupped her bare breasts, lifting them, kissing them. "I'd rather have you ask," he said, his breath cool on her hot, wet skin, "than wonder and imagine the worst." He sucked a nipple into his mouth.

"That's one," she breathed, clinging to his shoulders.

"One what?"

"Weak spot."

"Mmm." He tended to the needs of the other. "And is this . . . too?"

She arched into him. "Oh! Yes!"

"Shell?"

"Hmm?" She opened her eyes and realized she was lying on her back on an enormous bed and had no clear memory of having got there. Jase knelt over her, his hands on either side of her, his knees bracketing her hips.

His eyes were black with emotion. "I never meant to fall in love with you."

Slowly, concentrating hard, she undid his shirt buttons. "Did you?" She parted the shirt and slid her hands over the thick dark hair that curled over his chest. "Fall in love with me?"

He smiled and brushed the lightest of kisses over her lips. "Oh, yes. Very much so." He flopped down to lie beside her, one arm over his eyes.

"After Sterling accused me and I admitted it, and you looked at me as if I were the lowest scum on earth, I wanted to sit down and bawl like a little kid, because you hated me. In that moment I knew I loved you. You don't know how close I came to blowing my entire case before I even have one."

She pulled his arm down and leaned over him, trailing one finger through the thick hair on his chest. She fiddled with a nipple and kissed it, then sat back to admire the result. The bruises that had been so livid only four days earlier were now pale yellow around the edges and several shades of hideous green in the center.

"Do you have a case?" she asked, and her voice wobbled.

Jase hurt for her. "The message read, 'We have a match.' I'll be getting enlargements tomorrow."

Her shoulders heaved once as she sat up and dropped her head to his chest. "Poor Grandma."

He enfolded her with love, rocked her with compassion and tenderness. "I know, my darling. I know how bad it makes you feel."

She leaned back, her eyes glistening with unshed tears, and traced the shape of his lips with her finger. *His* grandmother hadn't had a hero to prevent the villain from tying her to the railroad tracks. And Jase still suffered because of that. "Yes," she said. "You do know, don't you?"

He nodded. "That's why I have to stop him."

She swallowed. "Jase . . . make love with me. Please."

"So you can forget?"

She smiled weakly. "No. Because I ache with wanting you, and I'm not sure how to get things going. None of what I've done so far seems to have worked."

He laughed and shoved her hand down to the front of his trousers. "It's worked, darlin'. Believe me, it's worked. But I always seem to be rushing you. I didn't want to scare you again."

"I'm not scared. Or, if I am, it's only because I'm not very experienced, and maybe I won't . . . please you."

A flare of alarm lit his eyes. "You're not a virgin!"

"No. But . . ." —she smiled wryly—"I've never been to China."

His warmth engulfed her as he held her close,

and she nearly sobbed aloud at the incredible sensation of his bare skin against hers, his chest hair abrading her nipples, his heat invading her breasts. "Mai-Lee was a long time ago," he said. "I loved her when I was a very young sailor. I loved her, married her, brought her home with me. She . . . betrayed me the next time I was on sea duty. She left me for another man. I stopped loving her. Now, I love you."

Shell lifted her head. "End of story?"

He smiled. "No. Beginning of story." She kissed him until he groaned and pulled away. "May I make love to you now?"

"Haven't you been?"

"Not the way I want to." He sat up, tilted her back, and lifted her hips to pull her jeans and bikini panties off. His mouth followed the garments all the way to her feet, where he paused and kissed her toes before working his way back up. He kissed her breasts, molded them, took gentle and not-so-gentle bites of her neck, and wrapped his hand tenderly around her throat in that unique and madly arousing way he had while he took her mouth, making it his own territory to plunder as he chose.

Shell ached deep inside, filled with a terrible yearning. She shifted her legs against his, twisted them around his, then struggled to undo his pants and slide them off him. Rolling to a half-sitting position, she forced his pants down over his knees and feet, then kissed her way back up, as he had done. She lingered at his injury on his thigh, where only a small bandage remained, then traced up the inside of his thigh to the edge of his bulging underwear. She laid her cheek on that and released a shuddering breath.

He caught her, pulling her high against his chest, then wrapped her tightly in his arms and legs and rolled her under him. He pinned her legs with his, and his breath rasped against her neck as he spread her hair out over the pillow. "Woman . . . you're going to be deadly when you have what you think is enough experience."

"I want to start getting it. Now, Jase! Now!"

Her undulating hips seemed to urge him on, and she didn't try to quell them. Her low moans broke like waves over her ears as she lost herself in the sensations his caresses created. She pleaded with him, raked his back with her nails, arched to his mouth and probing fingers. When she thought she could take no more, she took more, until he thrust back from her, readied himself, then knelt over her again, between her legs. He stroked her slick moistness with soft, delicate touches, watching her face as she stared at him.

"Jase . . . please," she begged again, writhing beneath him. He gave in, sinking down over her, entering her with exquisite slowness at first. She surged up, though, and he drove hard, again and again, taking her completely, forcefully, and her world shattered around her.

"Sweetheart?" Long moments later he nuzzled her neck and shook his head, his hair tickling her chin.

"Hmm?"

"I'm sorry. I meant for that to be slow and sweet and to last forever. I rushed you again, didn't I?"

She laughed softly as she played with his earlobe. "I didn't mind. Maybe next time will be slow and sweet and will last forever."

Next time? At her words Jase felt himself grow and harden inside her. It had been good enough for her that she was already anticipating a next time? He kissed her very, very quickly, restraining himself with all the strength he had left.

"It will be," he said. "I promise you that, my darling. But now I have to leave you for a minute." She let her arms fall limply to the bed as he eased out of her carefully. "We don't want any spills or other accidents," he said, turning his back for a moment.

"I'd like to have your baby." Her words surprised even her, and her eyes were wide as he stared at her over his shoulder. "I mean . . . well, sort of as a hypothetical exercise in . . . in . . . speculation. If I was ever going to have a baby, I wouldn't mind if it was yours."

He lay beside her again and drew her close, pulling the covers over them. "Honey, babies aren't hypothetical. I'd never have one . . . on spec. I don't suppose I'll ever become a father. My life doesn't lend itself to that kind of self-indulgence."

She traced the line of one scar as it crossed his back from shoulder blade to armpit. "That's right," he said, as if she had asked. "I hate the idea of a widow and fatherless children weeping over my grave."

There was nothing she could say. Nothing she could do. Except kiss him.

"Don't I remember something about a promise?" she asked several minutes later as she listened to the heavy hammering of his heart, felt the hard, insistent prodding of his erection against her thigh. "Something about slow and sweet and lasting for . . . a long time?"

Jase didn't correct her memory of the words he'd used so carelessly.

Nothing lasted forever. Nothing.

But this time their lovemaking lasted for a long, long time.

There was something deliciously decadent, Shell thought the next morning, about stepping into a hotel elevator with a man after a night of making love, and going downstairs for breakfast. It made her feel even more wantonly wicked than the room-service breakfast in bed he had suggested would have. Were people looking at them, she wondered, taking their linked hands as proof that they were lovers? She liked having the world see her as Jase's lover.

And there was something decidedly embarrassing, she thought two hours later, about walking into her grandmother's apartment with that same man; they were no longer hand in hand, but Shell suspected that her grandmother would know without being told that she and Jase were lovers. Would she approve?

Especially after she heard what Jase had to tell her.

Evelyn Landry, a small, aristocratic-looking woman whose smooth, soft skin and erect bearing belied her age, met them at the door.

"Good morning, dear," she said after a moment

of clear astonishment at seeing Jase with Shell. She kissed her granddaughter on the cheek, gave Jase a cool nod, then addressed Shell as if Jase did not exist.

"I thought you'd be alone," she said, a faint admonition in her tone. "You asked me to be alone when you called this morning."

Shell clenched her fists inside her jacket pockets. "Yes, Grandma. I know. But . . ." She slid an uneasy look at her companion. "Jase is the one who has something to tell you, something you must know."

"Oh?" Evelyn smiled bleakly and flicked another dismissing glance at Jase. "And what might that be? Exactly how he intends to write about my son and attempt to destroy his career? Does he want to try to justify his deeds, or does he hope I'll give him some dirt out of my son's distant past?" She waved Shell to silence when she tried to answer what had been a purely rhetorical question.

"Sterling told me, you see," Evelyn went on, "what happened last night in your father's office. He is most disturbed at having been the one to hurt you by exposing this man for what he really is, but now that you know, I fail to understand why he is in your company. And in my home."

She spared Jase one more glance of outright condemnation, then continued. "I must say, Shell, when you called and asked to see me alone, I believed you were heartbroken at having been taken in by a false charmer and were seeking solace from me. Never did I expect you to arrive with the—the enemy himself at your side. I trust you can explain yourself adequately?"

"Grandma, please. Jase isn't the false charmer."

Evelyn's fine, fair brows rose toward her lightly tinted hair. "Oh? Your intonation suggests that there *is* a false charmer in our midst. Who might that be?"

"Sterling, Grandma." Shell took her grandmother's hand and led her into the living room. "Please, sit down and listen to us. You have to hear this, as much as I hate to be the one to tell you. Sterling is a con artist. He will hurt you if we let him. In fact, he's not Sterling Graves at all. Jase hasn't learned yet what name he was born with, but he can prove to you that he isn't Sterling Graves. It's Sterling Jase is after, not Dad—that was just a blind."

Evelyn sat erect on her rose brocade love seat. Only a faint tremor in her loosely linked hands betrayed that she was not as serene as she seemed to be. Shell sat beside her, covering Evelyn's hands with one of her own. "Please, Grandma? Will you listen? It's for your own—"

Evelyn sighed. "For my own good, dear? When you've lived as long as I, you learn that things given us for our own 'good' normally taste vile."

"No, ma'am," Jase said, speaking for the first time. "Not for your own good. For your own safety is the way I'd put it. May I sit down?"

Evelyn assented with a regal inclination of her head.

Jase took the matching chair opposite the love seat and set his laptop computer on the coffee table. He opened its lid and switched it on. It hummed to life. Luckily, only the battery connection had suffered from getting damp, and after it had dried out, it worked perfectly. He wished he could say the same for his briefcase. Being in the front seat, it had been completely immersed, and most of the paper inside had been reduced to a sodden mass of illegible ink on useless papier-mâché.

One item that had survived, however, was his grandmother's photo of Martin Francis. While his computer went through its initial warm-up phases, he pulled the snapshot from its new plastic case and handed it to Evelyn. "This man lived in Florida two years ago. His name, as you can see written on the back, was not Sterling Graves at that time."

Evelyn looked, turned the photo over, and stared at the picture again. "This man has no mustache." She lifted her eyes to Jase's. "But I must say he does bear a striking resemblance to Sterling."

Jase nodded and withdrew two folded sheets of paper from his pocket. They had arrived at his hotel early that morning. He passed her one. "This is an enlarged photograph of the prints from the right index finger and the right thumb of the man in that photograph." He handed her the other sheet. "And these are the prints I lifted last night off a glass Sterling Graves had handled. I took Polaroid photographs of them and faxed the results to a . . . friend in California. He made the comparisons and declared a match. He's an expert, but I believe the similarities are enough for even the untrained eye to see."

He showed several points of similarity, and

Evelyn sighed almost inaudibly as she set the papers on the coffee table.

"I went to school with Sterling's sister," she said, but her voice lacked strength. "I knew him, although he was somewhat younger. He—" She frowned and waved her hand over the photo, not looking at it. "That man knows many details of my girlhood."

Jase nodded. "Yes, ma'am. I know he does. He's very thorough." He turned the computer to face her, then knelt on the floor so he could show her different pieces of information as they came up on the screen at his command.

"Sterling Graves, the real one, passed away more than thirty years ago. This is an outline of his life, taken from documents I was able to obtain. He never married, fathered no children."

Jase pressed a button, and the screen was filled with a new file. "His sister, the one who was your high school and college friend, also died young—of cancer when she was in her early forties." That information was given in greater detail. Evelyn stared at it for several moments, then looked up.

"I see," she said. "Then he knew he was quite safe in using that name." She sighed again. "Why did he lie to me? What is his purpose?"

"He's a con man, Grandma," Shell said. "He wants your money."

"Yes. What else would a man want from someone of my age?"

"Grandma, you're a—"

Evelyn patted Shell's hand. "Hush, dear. Forgive me my moment of self-pity. It was foolish of me."

She straightened her spine and addressed Jase. "What do you want from me?"

"Help, Mrs. Landry, if you can bring yourself to do it. I suspect that Sterling—we'll continue to call him that, if you have no objections—will be asking you to withdraw securities and hand them over to him, temporarily, of course, so that he can gain enough evidence to convict an officer of the bank that employs him. That seems to be the story he uses most often."

"Then I'm not the first." Evelyn seemed to take some comfort in that.

"No, ma'am. What I'd like to see is that you're the last. I'm hoping you'll go along with him when he asks you to help him, or asks you for money on any pretext, and will let me know so I can catch him in the act."

Evelyn sat even straighter. "He's already asked. Naturally, I said that I would speak to my son first. He asked me not to do that. He made it sound very . . . plausible, the need for secrecy."

"Oh, Grandma," Shell whispered, sliding her arm around her grandmother's rigid back. "I'm so sorry. But don't worry. Jase can . . . I'm sure Jase can get back what you've lost." She gazed appealingly at him. "You see, he works for the FBI and—"

"Shell!" Evelyn shook off her arm and rounded on her. "What do you think I am, a stupid old woman? I merely said that Sterling asked me to help him in his investigations, not that I had done so. For goodness' sake! Your grandfather taught me much better than that."

She snorted in a very genteel and ladylike manner. "The idea that I'd sign over power of attorney, as Sterling requested, without a great deal more than the say-so of one charming man! I told him we'd discuss it after the holiday season, that business, even bank business, could wait until I'd properly celebrated the birth of Jesus."

Jase laughed aloud, and she turned to look at him. "What do you want me to do, young man?" she asked briskly. "And shouldn't the Mounties be in on this? I'm sure the FBI has no jurisdiction in Canada."

"No, Mrs. Landry. It doesn't. But what Shell forgot to tell you is that I'm on leave of absence from the FBI, not carrying a badge. My being here is strictly unofficial."

She raised her elegant eyebrows again, and Jase had a glimpse of what Shell might look like in fifty years. He wasted a moment regretting that he would not be around to see her then, then told himself he had no time for regrets. He had to live for the hour, the day, and snatch what happiness he could along the way.

"Indeed?" Evelyn's manner frosted up again. "Then if this is not an official investigation, why are we having this discussion?" She reached for the telephone. "If what you say is true, then the authorities must be brought in at once."

"Please." His single word stayed her hand. "I have the backing of my superiors in the FBI, and I promise you, if and when I have enough evidence to show the RCMP, assuming a crime has been committed in this country, they will have it. I'm doing this on my own because my grandmother was the one who took that photograph and wrote the name Martin Francis on the back of it."

He paused to control his voice, then added, "She took it a few months before he relieved her of her life's savings and left her to die alone."

"Ahh . . ." Understanding flooded Evelyn's face. "I see. I'm very sorry, er, Jase. And of course I'll help."

"Thank you. But I want it clearly understood right up front that if things go wrong, you risk losing a good deal of money. As long as this is not an official investigation, I can make no guarantees."

He smiled at Shell. "Even though your granddaughter seems to think of me as an invincible hero."

"That," Evelyn said, "is the way it should be." She patted Shell's hand again, then leaned forward. "All right, Jase. Where do we start? How do we perform this . . . I believe it's called a 'sting'?"

Jase stood, then bent down and kissed her on the cheek. "Mrs. Landry, *you* are a hero."

"Of course I am, young man. I only hope my acting is as good as Sterling's has been." For just a moment she faltered and looked elderly, frail, and stricken. "I really believed he cared for me."

Shell hugged her tightly. There were no words of comfort she could give. She was only grateful that Jase had come before her grandmother was put through the same kind of hurt and humiliation his had suffered.

It was good to have a hero on their side.

Ten

"I have never had a better New Year's Eve in my life," Jase said as he kissed Lil on the cheek. It was half-past midnight, thirty minutes into the new year, and he was stuffed with good food, high on great conversation, and hoarse from singing. "Thank you, all of you, for letting me be part of your family, and for the most wonderful holiday season I've ever spent." He included Shell, Maureen, Nola—and even Ned—in his smile as he slid an arm around Shell's shoulders.

"It's been a good day for me too," Lil said, reluctantly letting Maureen help her off the piano bench and into her chair. Then, in a flurry of hugs, kisses, and "good nights," he and Shell were out of the house and on the path, the flashlight beam bouncing between them as they ran through the silver rain toward her cottage.

The cottage had that same wonderful, welcoming warmth Jase had learned to associate with

Shell's home. Inside, he swept her into his arms and hummed one of the love songs they'd been singing with Lil and Maureen. Dipping and swaying, drunk on wine and joy, they danced around the kitchen. When Skeena jealously thrust her head between them, they fell, laughing, onto a chair never meant to hold more than one.

Jase adjusted Shell on his lap, shoved the dog's wet, cold nose away, and concentrated on wishing Shell a thorough happy New Year. "Happy New Year, ear," he said, and kissed that.

"Happy New Year, nose." He slid her down until she nearly lay across his legs and undid her jacket, then her blouse. "Oh, what have we here? Happy . . . Happy . . . Happy New Year, nipples, and ribs, and tummy, and . . . skirt? I don't want to wish your skirt a happy New Year," he complained. "I want to—"

"I want to go to bed," she interrupted in an urgent whisper. Pulling his head away from her belly, she sat up, then held him still for her kisses, angling her mouth across his, speaking against his lips. "I more than want to go to bed. I need to, Jase."

His eyes filled with mirth. "With me?"

"Of course with you!" She giggled. "What did you think I meant, alone? I've forgotten what it's like to sleep alone."

"Complaining?"

"Never." She nestled close. She hadn't been to bed alone in nearly two weeks. And if she had her way, she'd never go to bed without Jase at her side for as long as she lived.

"Oh, well. If I have to, I have to." He picked her

up and carried her to her room, kicking the door
shut on the dog who would have joined them.

"You mean 'A man's gotta do,' etc.?"

He let out a long-suffering sigh. "Being a man
isn't easy, you know. Especially with you around.
You deliberately make things hard for me."

She giggled and made things harder.

He looked into her eyes, and she saw something
so deep and dark and mysterious, it half frightened her. "I love you, Shell." He set her down on
the bed and knelt beside her.

"I love you, Jase."

"I want to do things to you that have never been
done before, make you feel things you've never
even dreamed you could feel, show you ecstasy
you never imagined existed."

"You have done all that."

"But there's more. I'm sure of it. I think, together, we can find it."

She lay back and stretched her arms high over
her head. "Show me, then," she said. "Ah . . .
yes. Yes!"

"And you show me," he said in that special low
growl of his that told her he was deeply aroused.
"Show me the way to heaven."

She did.

An hour later Shell stretched again, languidly,
and smiled at him. "I believe you."

He followed the curve of her hipbone with a
finger, then traced a long, circuitous route to the
point of her jaw. "About what?"

"That you love me."

His nose wrinkled. "Oh, that." He shrugged,

then bent to kiss the last place his finger had touched.

"Shell?" He sat back and looked at her, his face too serious.

"Yes?"

"That's what I want to say."

She blinked. "What do you want to say?"

"Yes."

"Jase?" She shook her head, searching his eyes for any glint of humor that might be lurking there. There was none that she could see. "Is this conversation supposed to make sense?"

"Yes."

"You already said that."

A tiny smile played at the corners of his mouth. "Then you're supposed to say 'Thank you.'"

"Oh. Thank you." Quiet, sweet, precious moments passed. "What am I thanking you for?"

"For saying yes."

She was silent for a minute. "I seem to have forgotten the question."

"No wonder. You asked it so long ago. Twenty-three-and-a-half years ago, to be exact."

She went very still, then hitched herself up against the headboard and folded her arms on her knees. "What question, *to be exact*?"

"Well, maybe it was more of a statement than a question. You said, 'When we're all grown up, we'll get married, and you can kiss me, and we'll have lots of babies.' I'm simply agreeing with your suggestion. A little late, maybe, but very, very sincerely."

She drew in a breath, but it didn't help. She still felt light-headed, floating. She let it out and tried another one. Maybe the first one had missed the oxygen somehow. It hadn't. Maybe there was no more oxygen in the room. "Jase?"

"Marry me, Shell. Have my babies. Make a home for me. With me."

She wanted to weep, but she wouldn't. She wanted to believe him, believe he'd still feel this way a week from now, a month, a year, but she couldn't. "You're feeling sentimental, that's all," she said gently, sadly. "Christmas trees, prettily wrapped presents, your stocking."

Lil had filled a stocking for him, and he'd been more than slightly touched by the kindness. He hadn't had a Christmas stocking since he was five years old, he'd told them. Lil and Shell had both cried over that. Even Maureen's nose had turned red, and she'd rushed to the kitchen to do something to the turkey.

"New Year's Eve makes people mourn the passing of the season," Shell said, after Jase had shaken his head to each of her suggestions.

"This," he reminded her, "is New Year's Day."

"But . . . " She searched his eyes. "Those fatherless children you don't want weeping over your grave. What about them, Jase?"

He brushed her hair back from her face. "I want to see them grow up. A tall, thin blond boy who'll look like your father. A little girl who'll look just like you. Maybe two or three of those. And another, who looks like me. A boy who might resemble your mother, but in a masculine way. Maybe a couple who'd have your grandmother's courage, or one or two with the characteristics of—"

"How many little children do you anticipate

hanging over your grave? That sounds like about a dozen to me."

"Oh. Too many? But we'd have so much fun making them. And as for the grave scene, I've scratched it. Like I said, I want to watch our children grow up. I can make my leave of absence permanent, Shell."

She stared at him. "And do what? Write nasty little stories for a nasty little newspaper, so that nasty, small-minded people can get their jollies reading them?" She heard the shrillness in her tone and hated it, but she hated more the idea of his doing that. He had to know. If he really wanted to marry her, he had to know how she felt about that.

Oh, dear God. He would also have to know why. She clamped a hand over her mouth.

"I'll only write nasty stories about nasty people, never about nice one." His smile told her he was teasing. He nuzzled her hand away from her mouth with his chin and planted a loud, wet kiss on her lips. "Please, Shell. What I do and where I do it is immaterial as long as I can have you in my life."

"Your column, though. It may have started out as a cover for your other activities, but you've made a success out of it, haven't you? You won't want to give it up, not if you give up the FBI too."

He sat back from her. "I'm telling you," he said with exaggerated patience, "it doesn't matter what I do. I can wash cars, or wait tables, or dung out chicken coops. I don't have to work for a newspaper if it bothers you. I love you. I want to grow old beside you. I want those babies you promised me all those years ago. And I want you. Not just for a long time. I'm looking for something pretty damned close to forever. I'm saying yes, Shell. Now, please, please, say what you have to say."

She pulled in a tremulous breath, hesitated, then said, "Thank you."

Jase let out a whoop that made Skeena bark excitedly right outside the door, then he hauled Shell back down flat on the bed.

"Jase, don't," she said. "There's so much we have to talk about."

He grinned. "Oh, right! There is one very important thing. I will never, ever, as long as I live, agree to eat a spaghetti-sauce sandwich."

She pretended a huff. "Sorry. You'll learn to like them or it's no deal."

He laughed and kissed her with dizzying intensity.

"Jase, please, wait. We have to be serious. We need to talk."

"I don't want to wait. And I'm very serious. It's just that I don't want to talk. We can spend our golden years doing that, and watching *Wheel of Fortune* if you like, but right now what we have to do is make love. Make babies."

She laughed and clung to him. He was right. Now was not the time for talk. Now was the time for love. Details could be sorted out later.

"You look pretty busy, Madame Proprietor," Jase said, leaning in the doorway of Shell's back room. She looked up from the box of books she was unpacking and tried to leap to her feet and fly into his arms. Just seeing him after a three-day separation, though, turned her weak and limp with need, a need that couldn't be assuaged there in her store.

She remained crouched where she was, knowing her face was a complete giveaway of her feelings anyhow. Jase had told her repeatedly over the past three weeks that she couldn't hide her love. She didn't see any reason to try.

"How's Grandma?" she asked, when the strength finally returned to her legs and she could stand. She lifted the box to a table and stood looking at the man she loved. The smile she couldn't contain beamed forth. "Oh, Jase, I'm so glad to see you! I wasn't expecting you until the five-thirty ferry."

"I missed you so bad I caught the three-thirty, and Grandma's fine." He came fully into the room and shut the door, then perched one hip on the corner of her desk. His smile faded.

"We got a tape of Sterling discussing his 'case' with Evelyn. Shell, she's a phenomenal actress. No one would ever guess that she knew he was up to no good, or that she wasn't just as enamored of him as she was before Christmas. She gave him those phony documents your dad prepared. As soon as he tries to leave the country with them, or cash them in, we'll have him dead to rights. Your dad has customs officers watching for him at every border point Sterling could conceivably use, and every major financial institution in both countries is on the alert."

"Good." Her voice shook with passion. "I want to see him go to jail for the rest of his natural life."

Jase smiled crookedly. "Your grandmother and I have agreed that hanging would be appropriate."

"Yes, well, we have to take what the law provides."

He nodded, but not happily. "You and Evelyn were right, you know. It was a good move to bring Elwin in on this. He and Sondra are being wonderfully supportive of her."

"Oh, Jase, I should be there too. Are you sure she's all right?"

"She's more angry than sad now, Shell. And she's one very tough lady. You know that. I've promised her that we'll come and visit her in a few weeks, after she goes back to Palm Springs. Call her, why don't you? Talk to her for a minute or two, put your mind at rest."

"But . . . what if Sterling's there? It might be hard for her to talk normally."

"Yeah. That's true. And speaking of hard . . ." He grinned. "Can we get out of here soon and go home?"

Shell's insides rippled, and she glanced at her watch. "Soon. It's almost closing time. I just want to finish unpacking this box and getting the books onto the shelves." As she spoke, she continued to take books out. She glanced at their jackets, dusted them off, and set them on the cart beside her. "It's an order that should have been here before Christmas but got held up somewhere," she said as she found the invoice and began checking off titles.

"It's really frustrating when that happens," she went on, "because sales are never as brisk in January and Februa—" She broke off and stared at the back cover of a book as she lifted it from the box. Then she looked up at Jase, her face drained of color, her lips parted on the word she hadn't completed.

"Jase . . . " She glanced down at the jacket photo, back at him, and repeated his name. "Jase."

He knew what she held. "Oh, Shell, sweetheart—"

Her eyes burned into his. "Jason Calhoun," she said. "*When Angels Fall.*" She read aloud the copy above his picture. "'Shocking exposés by former FBI agent.' 'A must-read for anyone who wants the down-and-dirty on the televangelist scandals.' 'Calhoun judges the judges; finds more wrongdoing in court than out.'" She stared at him. "Jase! You wrote this—this trash? This slime?" He reached for her as her face crumpled, but she shoved him away with furious strength.

"That picture!" She slapped her hand over it, hiding it from her sight. "That was it! That was why I associated your face with a camera, but it was a promotional photograph I remembered, not you, not the boy I knew. The jacket—"

"Shell, listen to me!"

"No!" she shouted. "I don't want to hear anything you have to say! You're a liar, Jase! A cheat! You know how I feel about this kind of muck! Of course that's why you didn't tell me. Oh, sure you don't mind quitting the FBI. You can always find something else to do. I don't like your column? You'll quit that too? No problem, right?"

She ran an agitated hand through her hair and sobbed once, harshly. "Why would there be a problem when you have something so much better to turn to, some way to earn so much more money with your poison, your filth, your lies?"

She slammed the book down hard on the table. "This way you can destroy lives and reputations on a much bigger scale! Right, Jase? Right? Eat people for breakfast wholesale! Run their lives through the wringer of your printing presses, squeezing out every little detail that might titillate the jaded interest of every small-minded, sleaze-loving cretin in the Free World! Why limit your audience to southern California? Go national! International! Make a really big splash in the sewer! Right?"

Suddenly, he was as angry as she was. "No, dammit, wrong! I don't destroy lives! I write only the truth! That book evolved out of my columns, was requested by the publisher because he saw value in what I wrote."

"Value?" She picked up the book again and read aloud. " 'The down-and-dirty'? There's value in that?"

"I'm not responsible for the damned jacket copy. I'm not responsible for lurid reviewers' quotes. I'm only responsible for what's between the covers, and that I can vouch for. Every word I wrote is true, and the people I wrote about are the ones who destroy lives, not me. Why shouldn't the world know? It may protect the innocent in the future!"

"Bull!" She flung the book at him, and it skipped across the top of the desk, bounced off the wall, and landed faceup on the floor. "That's what you all say, you manure peddlers! You cite the public's right to know as if it were some kind of mantra. What about the rights of the innocent? What about the rights of people who don't want to see their dirty linen spread out for everyone to view? What about the rights of the families of those men you attack? Don't they have the right not to be hurt, not to be smeared, not to see their loved ones destroyed by your poison?

"Get out, Jason O'Keefe, or Calhoun, or whatever the hell your name really is. Get out of my store and out of my life. I never want to see you again!"

"Oh, you've got it, lady. No problem! I'm outta here. And I'll take my offenses with me."

He picked up the book, took a handful of cash from his pocket and tossed it to the floor where the book had lain, then turned on his heel and left, slamming the door behind him.

"Shirl, darling, you have to stop crying sometime, you know. You've been at it for nearly three weeks."

Shell wiped her eyes and sat up, dredging up a smile for her mother. "That's not true. I don't cry all the time, Lil. I haven't cried for days. Until this afternoon." She'd come home from work an hour earlier and succumbed to the tears she'd been fighting all day. PMS, she'd told herself, but she knew that wasn't true. She'd had her period a week earlier. She'd have no little child to weep over her grave, and she'd cried about that for the better part of a night. "And I never cry at work."

"Well, you certainly do a lot of it at home," Lil

said briskly, "and I'm getting weary of it. Are you ready to tell me what went wrong?"

Shell straightened the book catalogs on her desk, squaring them with the corner. "It simply wasn't meant to be." Stubbornly, she clung to the phrase she'd used since the day she'd thrown Jase out.

"Would it have something to do with this?" Lil pulled a tabloid from the folds of the blanket covering her knees.

LILIANNE MURDERED, the headline screamed. Then:

> Twenty years after the disappearance of the most beautiful woman in the world, her former lover finally admits to the slaying. "I killed her," says the ghost of Maximillian Elkford, confessing from beyond the grave through channeler Andrea Kiminski, a Santa Monica housewife and medium. Elkford, who died of AIDS three years ago (*see p. 3: Lilianne*)

"Oh, Mom!" Shell took the paper and tore it in two, then in two again, tossing it to the floor in disgust. "We knew this would happen. Lord, how I hate them!" She shoved her hands into her hair. "Why can't they leave us alone?"

"Because I was public property for so long, dear. But is that what's bothering you, or is it this?" This time Lil held out a book—*the book*—and Shell crumpled. "Honey, are you afraid for me? Do you think Jase would try to make money on me?"

Shell buried her face in her mother's lap. "Why not?" she moaned. "He's willing to make money on anybody else he can exploit. He's a reporter! It's his nature. He can't change that."

"No. And you're paranoid about newspapers, but I believe we *can* change that." Shell heard her mother breathe in long and deep and looked up. "Jase knows who I am, Shirl. I told him."

She sat back on her heels and stared, horrified, at Lil. "You did what?"

"I told him. He has my written permission to tell the world."

"No! Good Lord, no! You know what will happen! They'll be here in hordes. They'll never let you rest! We'll be inundated! Oh, Lil, why?"

"Because you gave him up out of fear, Shirl."

"No. Out of necessity."

"Fear." Lil was quietly adamant. "It's a fear that I should have taken from you, darling. This is all my fault. But when I first became ill, having the truth come out seemed worse to me, a crueler fate than the ugly speculation I had to suffer. I thought I couldn't bear seeing pity where once there had been adoration.

"But now . . ." she smoothed Shell's hair. "Now I'm much older, much wiser, and so very much stronger."

Shell shook her head, unable to release the fears and beliefs she'd lived with for more than twenty years. "No! No, you're not. The stress of having them hound you would be bad, Mom. What does Maureen say? She can't want you to do this any more than I do."

"That's right, she doesn't."

"Then don't."

"But I have to. You'll never go to the man you

love unless you can do it without fear of exposing me."

Shell was heartsick. "Then you'd be doing it for me and not for yourself."

Lil smiled sweetly. "Why not, darling? I've remained hidden for you for all these years."

Shell sat back. "For me? No, Lil." She shook her head again. "No."

"Oh, I'm not blaming you," Lil said. "I remember how it was. I remember falling down and not being able to get up. I remember the slurred speech, the failing vision that made me stumble and run into things, the collapsing limbs that everyone believed meant I was turning into a drunk. I remember how bad it was, for both of us. But it was worse for you because you were a little child and didn't understand.

"You're not a child now, though, my darling. You're a grown woman, and you must face the world. If it spits on you, you have to get up and spit back. You can't cower the way I did. And I taught you to do that by my actions. Don't you see how wrong that was? I'm not going to hide any longer, and I won't let you, either. That's why I gave Jase my story. He was supposed to print it today. I expected to see it in all the major papers."

She smiled wryly and indicated the torn paper on the floor. "That, surprisingly, was the only article of note dealing with my disappearance. I guess I'm not as important as I thought."

Shell got to her feet. She paced across the room and looked out onto the fresh lumber of her new front porch. "If Jase had given your story to his editor, to any editor in the world, it would have been published."

"Then where do you suppose it is, Shirl? Why do you think it isn't in print?"

Shell turned, and she could scarcely speak for the tears clogging her throat. "Because he didn't give it to his editor."

"Do you have to ask why he didn't?"

"Oh, Mom." Shell sank to the couch, clutching fistfuls of the afghan that lay folded there. "I think I'm going to have to go to Los Angeles."

Lil smiled. "Your father's got your tickets. Your flight leaves at nine. If you hurry, you'll make the next ferry."

Shell gathered her mother close. "I love you, Lilianne."

"Good. Then be a big, brave girl and make your mama proud."

Jase took a bite, then set his sandwich down. It wasn't bad, but he wasn't hungry. He hadn't been hungry for a long time. He ate because he had to, because when he didn't, he got so grumpy nobody wanted to be around him. That wasn't so bad, really, because he didn't want to be around other people. But when he chose to, it would be nice if they'd be a bit sympathetic, instead of snarling at him because he snarled at them.

He took another bite and snarled at his sandwich when the doorbell rang. He wasn't expecting anyone. Maybe if he ignored whoever it was, he'd go away. But no. The last time he'd tried that, his buddy Ace had gotten the super to unlock the door. Jase's car was in the lot, and Ace had figured he'd done himself in.

Hah! Jase thought. The day he did himself in over a woman! That'd be the day! "Hah!" he said aloud as he snatched the door open.

"Hah?"

"Haaah . . ." He backed up several steps, not noticing that he had let his sandwich fall to the floor. He stepped on it, smearing a messy red splotch across the cream-colored carpet. He didn't notice until Shell said, "What in the world are you eating?"

He glanced down and wiped his bare foot on a clean area of the carpet. "Oh. That. A spaghetti-sauce sandwich."

She stared at him. "Why?"

"To . . . see what they're like. In case . . ." He frowned. "Nothing." He looked at her, at the bag she had slung over her shoulder, at the tears sliding down her face. "Why are you here?"

"Because I love you. Because I'm miserable without you. Because Lil . . . my mother, Lilianne, the former beauty queen and movie star whom Max Elkford did not murder twenty years ago, regardless of what his ghost says, told me I had to quit crying, but I can't stop, Jase, no matter how hard I try, and I do try and try, but the tears just keep leaking out, and pretty soon I'm going to dehydrate so bad I'll shrivel up and die, and I won't have even one little child to weep over my grave."

He looked at her for a long time, frowning. "Is any of that supposed to make sense?"

She sniffled. "Didn't it?"

He shook his head.

"Do I need to try again?"

He shook his head once more. "I don't think so. You and I . . . Well, maybe we're not supposed to make sense." He took a step toward her and walked in the squashed sandwich again. He wiped his foot off, dirtying another section of carpet.

"What—what are we supposed to make?" she asked fearfully.

"Love," he said, drawing her into his arms. "Just love."

Moments later he lifted his head and smiled at her. "Much as I'd like to continue kissing you, Shell, maybe that's where we've gone wrong. It feels so good to hold you, I don't want to think, don't want to talk. I just want to love you."

"I know. But there are things we have to discuss. Such as why you didn't sell Lil's story."

He led her to his sofa and sat down, still holding her, his right hand pulling her hair free from its ponytail and spreading it over her shoulders. Grinning wickedly, he said, "Now why would I want to do that? Lilianne's not a nasty. My readers wouldn't be interested in her unless she had some deep, dark, dirty secrets to impart, the juicier the better, the more ghastly and grisly the merrier, the more—"

"Stop. You've made your point." Shell toyed with a button on his shirt, staring at that rather than look at him. "Is it enough to say that I'm sorry? That I was wrong? I read your book, Jase. And I've looked up some of your columns. What you're doing isn't much different from what my dad did when he exposed that money-laundering scheme."

She glanced up for a second. "I'll grovel if that'll help."

"Hey." He tilted her chin up, sliding his hand around her throat, gently, tenderly. "You're here. That's all that matters. I could have told you the truth, but by the time I was ready to mention my column, I knew how you felt about newspapers and journalists." He looked ashamed for a moment as he went on. "I didn't tell you about the book because, well, this is going to sound conceited as hell, but it's gotten a fair bit of local publicity, and I've learned that there are people who . . . collect writers, people who didn't want to bother with me until they'd seen me on a talk show or two. I'm not comfortable with it. I prefer to be loved for who I am, not what I do."

She smiled and linked her hands behind his neck. "No kidding. Those people must be related to the ones who collect movie stars."

He nodded. "And their children. Lil told me how bad it was for you, sweetheart. And for her at the end. I don't blame you both for going into hiding." He rested his forehead against hers. "How 'bout we protect each other from the hounds?"

"I'm not going to hide anymore, Jase. And neither is Lil. She wanted you to publish your account of meeting her. She's ready to face the public again."

He leaned back and shook his head. "No. That story's not mine to sell. Or to tell. It's hers, and I hope to persuade *her* to make a book out of it. Don't you think it would be appropriate, the book appearing on the twenty-first anniversary of her disappearance? Sort of a coming-of-age time for the new Lilianne?"

"And a new maturity for little Shirley Elizabeth."

He pulled her close. "I think she's found that already."

"Jase?" Shell asked several minutes later. "Have we talked enough yet?"

"Hmm . . . yeah." He looked pained. "I guess that means I have to make love with you now."

She smiled. "And babies."

He shrugged. "A man's gotta do . . ."

THE EDITOR'S CORNER

Next month's lineup sizzles with BAD BOYS, heroes who are too hot to handle but too sinful to resist. In six marvelous romances, you'll be held spellbound by these men's deliciously wicked ways and daring promises of passion. Whether they're high-powered attorneys, brash jet jockeys, or modern-day pirates, BAD BOYS are masters of seduction who never settle for anything less than what they want. And the heroines learn that surrender comes all too easily when the loving is all too good. . . .

Fighter pilot Devlin MacKenzie in **MIDNIGHT STORM** by Laura Taylor, LOVESWEPT #576, is the first of our BAD BOYS. He and David Winslow, the hero of DESERT ROSE, LOVESWEPT #555, flew together on a mission that ended in a horrible crash, and now Devlin has come to Jessica Cleary's inn to recuperate. She broke their engagement years before, afraid to love a man who lives dangerously, but the rugged warrior changes her mind in a scorchingly sensual courtship. Laura turns up the heat in this riveting romance.

SHAMELESS, LOVESWEPT #577, by Glenna McReynolds, is the way Colt Haines broke Sarah Brooks's heart by leaving town without a word after the night she'd joyfully given him her innocence. Ten years later a tragedy brings him back to Rock Creek, Wyoming. He vows not to stay, but with one look at the woman she's become, he's determined to make her understand why he'd gone—and to finally make her his. Ablaze with the intensity of Glenna's writing, **SHAMELESS** is a captivating love story.

Cutter Beaumont *is* an **ISLAND ROGUE**, LOVESWEPT #578, by Charlotte Hughes, and he's also the mayor, sheriff, and owner of the Last Chance Saloon. Ellie Parks isn't interested though. She's come to the South Carolina island looking for a peaceful place to silence the demons that haunt her dreams—and instead she finds a handsome rake who wants to keep her up nights. Charlotte masterfully resolves this trouble in paradise with a series of events that will make you laugh and cry.

Jake Madison is nothing but **BAD COMPANY** for Nila Shepherd in Theresa Gladden's new LOVESWEPT, #579. When his sensual gaze spots her across the casino, Jake knows he must possess the temptress in the come-and-get-me dress. Nila has always wanted to walk on the wild side, but the fierce desire Jake awakens in her has her running for cover. Still, there's no hiding from this man who makes it his mission to fulfill her fantasies. Theresa just keeps coming up with terrific romances, and aren't we lucky?

Our next LOVESWEPT, #580 by Olivia Rupprecht, has one of the best titles ever—**HURTS SO GOOD**. And legendary musician Neil Grey certainly knows about hurting; that's why he dropped out of the rat race and now plays only in his New Orleans bar. Journalist Andrea Post would try just about anything to uncover his mystery, to write the story no one ever had, but the moment he calls her *"chère,"* he steals her heart. Another memorable winner from Olivia!

Suzanne Forster's stunning contribution to the BAD BOYS month is **NIGHT OF THE PANTHER**, LOVESWEPT #581. Johnny Starhawk is a celebrated lawyer whose killer instincts and Irish-Apache heritage have made him a star, but he's never forgotten the woman who'd betrayed him. And now, when Honor Bartholomew is forced to seek his help, will he give in to his need for revenge . . . or his love for the only woman he's ever wanted? This romance of smoldering anger and dangerous desire is a tour de force from Suzanne.

On sale this month from FANFARE are four terrific novels. **DIVINE EVIL** is the most chilling romantic suspense novel yet from best-selling author Nora Roberts. When successful sculptor Clare Kimball returns to her hometown, she discovers that there's a high price to pay for digging up the secrets of the past. But she finds an ally in the local sheriff, and together they confront an evil all the more terrifying because those who practice it believe it is divine.

HAVING IT ALL by critically acclaimed author Maeve Haran is a tender, funny, and revealing novel about a woman who does have it all—a glittering career, an exciting husband, and two adorable children. But she tires of pretending she's superwoman, and her search for a different kind of happiness and success shocks the family and friends she loves.

With **HIGHLAND FLAME**, Stephanie Bartlett brings back the beloved heroine of HIGHLAND REBEL. In this new novel, Catriona Galbraid and her husband, Ian, depart Scotland's Isle of Skye after they're victorious in their fight for justice for the crofters. But when a tragedy leaves Cat a widow, she's thrust into a new struggle—and into the arms of a new love.

Talented Virginia Lynn creates an entertaining variation on the taming-of-the-shrew theme with **LYON'S PRIZE**. In medieval England the Saxon beauty Brenna of Marwald is forced to marry Rye de Lyon, the Norman knight known as the Black Lion. She vows that he will never have her love, but he captures her heart with passion.

Sharon and Tom Curtis are among the most talented authors of romantic fiction, and you wouldn't want to miss this chance to pick up a copy of their novel **THE GOLDEN TOUCH**, which LaVyrle Spencer has praised as being "pure pleasure!" This beautifully written romance has two worlds colliding when an internationally famous pop idol moves into the life of a small-town teacher.

The Delaneys are coming! Once again Kay Hooper, Iris Johansen, and Fayrene Preston have collaborated to bring you a sparkling addition to this remarkable family's saga. Look for **THE DELANEY CHRISTMAS CAROL**—available soon from FANFARE.

Happy reading!

With best wishes,

Nita Taublib

Nita Taublib
Associate Publisher
LOVESWEPT and FANFARE

OFFICIAL RULES TO WINNERS CLASSIC SWEEPSTAKES

No Purchase necessary. To enter the sweepstakes follow instructions found elsewhere in this offer. You can also enter the sweepstakes by hand printing your name, address, city, state and zip code on a 3" x 5" piece of paper and mailing it to: Winners Classic Sweepstakes, P.O. Box 785, Gibbstown, NJ 08027. Mail each entry separately. Sweepstakes begins 12/1/91. Entries must be received by 6/1/93. Some presentations of this sweepstakes may feature a deadline for the Early Bird prize. If the offer you receive does, then to be eligible for the Early Bird prize your entry must be received according to the Early Bird date specified. Not responsible for lost, late, damaged, misdirected, illegible or postage due mail. Mechanically reproduced entries are not eligible. All entries become property of the sponsor and will not be returned.

Prize Selection/Validations: Winners will be selected in random drawings on or about 7/30/93, by VENTURA ASSOCIATES, INC., an independent judging organization whose decisions are final. Odds of winning are determined by total number of entries received. Circulation of this sweepstakes is estimated not to exceed 200 million. Entrants need not be present to win. All prizes are guaranteed to be awarded and delivered to winners. Winners will be notified by mail and may be required to complete an affidavit of eligibility and release of liability which must be returned within 14 days of date of notification or alternate winners will be selected. Any guest of a trip winner will also be required to execute a release of liability. Any prize notification letter or any prize returned to a participating sponsor, Bantam Doubleday Dell Publishing Group, Inc., its participating divisions or subsidiaries, or VENTURA ASSOCIATES, INC. as undeliverable will be awarded to an alternate winner. Prizes are not transferable. No multiple prize winners except as may be necessary due to unavailability, in which case a prize of equal or greater value will be awarded. Prizes will be awarded approximately 90 days after the drawing. All taxes, automobile license and registration fees, if applicable, are the sole responsibility of the winners. Entry constitutes permission (except where prohibited) to use winners' names and likenesses for publicity purposes without further or other compensation.

Participation: This sweepstakes is open to residents of the United States and Canada, except for the province of Quebec. This sweepstakes is sponsored by Bantam Doubleday Dell Publishing Group, Inc. (BDD), 666 Fifth Avenue, New York, NY 10103. Versions of this sweepstakes with different graphics will be offered in conjunction with various solicitations or promotions by different subsidiaries and divisions of BDD. Employees and their families of BDD, its division, subsidiaries, advertising agencies, and VENTURA ASSOCIATES, INC., are not eligible.

Canadian residents, in order to win, must first correctly answer a time limited arithmetical skill testing question. Void in Quebec and wherever prohibited or restricted by law. Subject to all federal, state, local and provincial laws and regulations.

Prizes: The following values for prizes are determined by the manufacturers' suggested retail prices or by what these items are currently known to be selling for at the time this offer was published. Approximate retail values include handling and delivery of prizes. Estimated maximum retail value of prizes: 1 Grand Prize ($27,500 if merchandise or $25,000 Cash); 1 First Prize ($3,000); 5 Second Prizes ($400 each); 35 Third Prizes ($100 each); 1,000 Fourth Prizes ($9.00 each) ; 1 Early Bird Prize ($5,000); Total approximate maximum retail value is $50,000. Winners will have the option of selecting any prize offered at level won. Automobile winner must have a valid driver's license at the time the car is awarded. Trips are subject to space and departure availability. Certain black-out dates may apply. Travel must be completed within one year from the time the prize is awarded. Minors must be accompanied by an adult. Prizes won by minors will be awarded in the name of parent or legal guardian.

For a list of Major Prize Winners (available after 7/30/93): send a self-addressed, stamped envelope entirely separate from your entry to: Winners Classic Sweepstakes Winners, P.O. Box 825, Gibbstown, NJ 08027. Requests must be received by 6/1/93. DO NOT SEND ANY OTHER CORRESPONDENCE TO THIS P.O. BOX.

The Delaney Dynasty lives on in

The Delaney Christmas Carol

by Kay Hooper, Iris Johansen, & Fayrene Preston

Three of romantic fiction's best-loved authors present the changing face of Christmas spirit—past, present, and future—as they tell the story of three generations of Delaneys in love.

CHRISTMAS PAST by Iris Johansen

From the moment he first laid eyes on her, Kevin Delaney felt a curious attraction for the ragclad Gypsy beauty rummaging through the attic of his ranch at Killara. He didn't believe for a moment her talk of magic mirrors and second-sight, but something about Zara St. Cloud stirred his blood. Now, as Christmas draws near, a touch leads to a kiss and a gift of burning passion.

CHRISTMAS PRESENT by Fayrene Preston

Bria Delaney had been looking for Christmas ornaments in her mother's attic, when she saw him in the mirror for the first time—a stunningly handsome man with sky-blue eyes and red-gold hair. She had almost convinced herself he was only a dream when Kells Braxton arrived at Killara and led them both to a holiday wonderland of sensuous pleasure.

CHRISTMAS FUTURE by Kay Hooper

As the last of the Delaney men, Brett returned to Killara this Christmastime only to find it in the capable hands of his father's young and beautiful widow. Yet the closer he got to Cassie, the more Brett realized that the embers of their old love still burned and that all it would take was a look, a kiss, a caress, to turn their dormant passion into an inferno.